Shandra H

Vanishing Dream

Shandra Higheagle Mystery
Book 16

Paty Jager

Windtree Press
Hillsboro, Oregon

Copyright

VANISHING DREAM

Special Thanks

This book and series are dedicated to my friend Carmen Peone who has given me the wings to write a series with a Native American character and for her help in making sure I depicted my character and the Colville Reservation correctly.

Chapter One

"I still don't understand why the kids have to meet
your family during the Powwow. There will be so many
people that they may feel overwhelmed. We could take
them to the ranch another time and let them meet
everyone slowly."

Shandra Higheagle Greer glanced over at her
husband, Ryan, driving their family to the Colville
Reservation in Washington. She knew he wasn't against
going to the Powwow, he was as protective as she was
of their recently adopted children. Shandra twisted her
head and neck to smile at the eight-year-old twins, Mia
and Jayden, in the back seat of the Jeep. They had been
upset Sheba, their big furry new friend, couldn't come,
but had been appeased when Shandra told them they
would be camping.

She returned her attention to Ryan. "Because of
Grandmother. She appeared in a dream with all of us
dancing at the powwow. There has to be a reason she

wishes us to attend." Even though her husband was skeptical about this trip, he'd been the first to believe in her dreams where Ella showed her clues to the murders they had solved together.

"I want to wear a dress that sounds like Santa's sleigh," Mia said.

"That's a jingle dress. We'll have to ask Aunt Jo if you can. Most girls your age who dance at a powwow have been learning the dance from a young age." Shandra was pleased their adopted twins were excited about learning a new culture. She'd shown them videos of past powwows to help them understand what they would be participating in.

"What do the boys dance?" Jayden asked.

"There are several dances for the boys. I'm sure my cousins, Coop and Andy, will be happy to teach you one of them." Shandra sent a blessing to the steel silhouettes of women digging for roots that stood along the highway on the Reservation. The "root diggers" as the cutouts were referred to by the locals, meant they would soon be coming upon the powwow grounds across the highway from the Agency gas station and market and not far from the community center where Aunt Jo worked.

Every time Shandra came to the reservation her soul yearned to learn more about her father's side of the family. Her Nez Perce heritage. This would be only the second powwow she'd participated in since learning her paternal family wanted her to be a part of their culture and family.

She was fortunate they all loved Ryan and respected her wish to learn more.

"I think camping at the powwow grounds with

everyone will make the experience that much more educational. If we stayed at the ranch, showing up in the morning and going back there at night, we wouldn't be able to share stories around the campfire and learn more about each of the family members." She smiled at Ryan when he glanced over at her.

"Are you sure you're ready to sleep on the thin padding we brought for under the sleeping bag?" Ryan asked.

He'd been questioning her wanting to camp. And with good reason. Since they'd met, they had never gone camping. As a child she'd slept out under the stars and stayed out overnight when looking for stray cattle, but she'd never had the full camping experience. Her stepfather hadn't been one to take vacations or do anything other than work.

"I am ready for an adventure." She glanced back at Jayden. "And Jayden told me that some of his best memories of his dad were when they went camping. That's what I want with my two families. You three and my aunts, uncles, and cousins."

The powwow grounds came into sight. "There, see the large round structure? That's the arbor where they do all the dancing."

Ryan switched on the left turn signal and drove onto the road leading to the powwow grounds. "Where do we find Aunt Jo and Uncle Martin?"

"She said the family always camps in the same area, two spots down from the vendors on the west side." Shandra scanned the area on the left side of the grounds and spotted her uncle's pickup. Her chest squeezed with anticipation and happiness. She felt like a kid for the first time in a really long time. "There! I see Uncle Martin's pickup. The red one."

There was a dusty, dry grass path that resembled a road, leading around the outside edge of the grounds. Ryan followed it until they were abreast of the red pickup. He parked. By the time the engine shut off her Aunt Jo, cousin Andy, and his daughter, Fawn, walked toward them from a group of teepees and a couple of tents.

Shandra exited the Jeep and hugged her aunt, Andy, and Fawn. "It's so good to see all of you."

"We have missed your visits but are excited you are spending Powwow week with us," Aunt Jo said, smiling.

Ryan and the twins joined them.

"Aunt Jo, Andy, Fawn, this is Mia and Jayden, the newest members of our family." Shandra put a hand on each of the children's shoulders.

"I'm so very happy to meet you," Aunt Jo said, shaking hands with each child. "This is my youngest son, Andy and his daughter, our granddaughter, Fawn. You'll meet Andy's older brother later in the week." Aunt Jo peered at Shandra. "Coop and Sandy are coming on Friday. He couldn't get away from work until then."

"The last time I talked to him, Coop sounded so happy." Her cousin had gone through a lot being thought of as a murder suspect and then thinking he'd lost the woman he loved. But he and Sandy were together and happy.

"He loves his job and his wife. But he does miss the reservation." Aunt Jo hugged Ryan. "We are happy you were able to spend the week as well."

Ryan grinned and pointed at Shandra. "I didn't

have a choice. She said we all had to be here."

"Yeah, she can be a bully," Andy said, moving backwards away from Shandra.

The twins and Fawn laughed.

"I'm not a bully."

A loud voice, and what sounded like something being thrown, tugged Shandra's attention away from Andy's teasing.

"I told you old lady, if you don't fix it, I will!" A man in his early thirties, dressed in jeans, an annual powwow t-shirt, and cowboy boots strode away from a woman, Shandra guessed to be in her seventies. The older woman wore a buckskin dress, beaded basket hat, and strings of beads around her neck. Her hair was white as snow and hung down her back in a long braid. The woman's expression couldn't be seen from the distance, but her hunched shoulders and slow gait proved she was sad.

"Who is that?" Shandra asked.

"Lucille Lightning. She makes the most authentic and gorgeous beadwork necklaces, purses and bags, moccasins and belts. You'll have to check out her work." Aunt Jo started herding them to the family camp area. "Andy, help Ryan get their stuff."

"I can help." Jayden peeled away from the females to join Ryan and Andy at the Jeep.

Shandra laughed. "Jayden is used to doing the job of a grownup. But he's also learning to be a child."

"What do you mean? He is a child," Mia said, stopping and staring at Shandra with confusion scrunching her face.

"You and your brother had to take care of yourselves a lot before your parents died. Jayden is still

11

trying to take care of you even though we keep telling him that is our job, he just needs to be a kid."

"And he took care of Mom—our aunt." The sadness in Mia's voice always tugged at Shandra's heart.

"Yes, he took care of everyone in your family. Including your dad. Now it's his turn to be taken care of." Shandra had fallen for the two before she knew their family circumstances. She'd witnessed them in a dream and knew in her heart she had to save them, however that may be. It turned out both their parents were murdered. She and Ryan became their foster parents to keep them safe, then adopted the pair because they were special.

"Want to see the teepee you'll be staying in?" Aunt Jo asked, bringing the child out of her sad memories.

"We're stayin' in a teepee? Wow! I'll have the best 'What I did this summer' story when we go back to school."

Shandra laughed. "I guess you will."

"Of course, this isn't as authentic as when the Nimiipuu were moving with the gathering of food, but it is a pretty good replica." Aunt Jo held the flap back on the teepee at the edge of the group of tents and teepees.

"Wow!" Mia said, walking in a circle, staring at the items Shandra was pretty sure were authentic from the days when her ancestors hunted and gathered.

"We didn't have any spare buffalo robes for you to use to sleep on. I hope these pads with woven blankets over them will keep you from feeling the hardness of the ground." Aunt Jo raised one of the smaller blankets to reveal a cot sized foam pad.

"They'll be more comfortable than the rolled-up yoga mats we brought." Shandra turned at the sound of her husband's voice.

"I'm impressed. I thought we'd be sleeping in a tent," Ryan stared at his wife. She hadn't been this animated since they'd found the children and adopted them.

"This is what I'd always dreamed of when I'd think about Daddy's side of the family," Shandra said, hugging her aunt.

Ryan dropped their sleeping bag and duffel of clothing on the double sized pad. "These pads look thicker than what we brought."

Jo laughed. "That's what Shandra said." She moved to where Jayden had dumped his and his sister's things. "This is your sister's bed. You may remain in here tonight. If you feel comfortable tomorrow, you may sleep with your boy cousins. It is where Andy and all the male cousins will be sleeping."

"But why would he sleep with boys and not with his daughter and wife?" Mia asked.

Shandra glanced at Fawn. She was Andy's daughter from a young woman who had used her body to get affection and ended up murdered. She and Ryan had helped solve her murder three years earlier when the child was four and Andy came forward to say he was the father.

"My mommy is dead. I stay with Grandma and Grandpa while Daddy stays with the boys." Fawn walked over to Andy and Jo, placing her hands in each one of theirs.

Knowing how protective Jayden was of his twin sister, Ryan doubted the boy would take Jo up on her offer.

"We tell stories, talk of what it means to become a man." Andy leaned down next to the boy and whispered something.

Jayden's eyes grew round and he grinned like he'd been told a good joke. "Really?"

"Yeah."

"What? What?" Mia asked.

Andy put a hand on Jayden's shoulder. "Sorry, it's for boys only. You'll get to do girl stuff tomorrow with Fawn and your girl cousins." Andy patted Jayden's shoulder. "See you at dinner."

Jayden's head bobbed like a bobblehead doll.

Ryan almost wished he were single the way the boy's eyes had lit up. Whatever they did in the boy's teepee must be fun.

Chapter Two

Once the sleeping bags had been spread out on the beds, with Jayden using everyone else's thin mat tonight as he remained in their teepee, and everything else hung from the sticks lashed to the teepee poles, Aunt Jo led them out to the center fire where more of Shandra's aunts were cooking the meal for tonight.

"Are you going to do any of the dances?" her cousin, Jackie, asked.

Shandra smiled. Her face heated. She'd been practicing a few of the dances from watching videos but she didn't have regalia. "I thought I would dance in the grand entry and any friendship dances."

"Do you have regalia?" another cousin, Skye, asked.

"I wasn't sure how authentic it needed to be, so no, I don't."

"She has been practicing the sleigh bell dance," Mia spoke up.

The grownups laughed.

"You mean the Jingle Dance," Aunt Jo corrected her.

"That one." Mia started dancing as they had been practicing. "I can do it, too."

"I see that." Aunt Jo peered at Shandra. "It seems we need to round up regalia for both of you." She shifted her gaze to Ryan and Jayden. "And what about you two?"

Ryan shook his head. "I will do the friendship dance. Unlike my wife and daughter, I haven't had time to practice any dances."

Aunt Jo nodded and studied Jayden. "And you?"

"I don't know if I want to or not. Dancing is for girls." Jayden glanced at Ryan as if wanting the man in his life to agree with him.

"You will learn when you sleep in the cousin teepee that dancing is good for the soul and grounds one's thoughts to your ancestors." Aunt Jo motioned to half a dozen children playing nearby. "Go play with the others until the meal is ready."

"We don't know them," the usually out-going Mia said, moving closer to Shandra.

"They are all cousins. Fawn is over there. You met her already. Walk over and introduce yourselves, and they will introduce themselves." Shandra smoothed the child's hair and crouched in front of her. "Remember how we talked about all the new experiences you would have here? Meeting other children could lead to a lifelong friendship." She grasped Mia's chin lightly. "Smile that friendly smile of yours and you'll be friends."

"Come on," Jayden said, staring hard at the group.

Shandra studied them and noticed they were playing a stick game.

Mia followed her brother, but glanced back over her shoulder a couple of times before they arrived at the group. It appeared Jayden made the introductions for himself and his sister. Fawn walked up to Mia and grasped her hand. They wandered over to the side and picked up a doll.

"They'll be fine. We told our children to welcome them," Jackie said, smiling.

"Thank you. They have gone through a lot in the last year," Shandra couldn't have felt any more maternal toward the twins if she'd birthed them.

Ryan kissed her temple. "Your uncle is signaling for me. I'll catch up with you later."

Shandra waved him off. "Go on. I'm sure they have man things for you to do."

He laughed and jogged over to where Uncle Martin, Andy, and two of her other uncles were sitting on upturned hunks of wood, talking.

"I thought he'd never leave," Aunt Jo said, her eyes twinkling.

"What are you up to?" Shandra asked, studying the mirth in her aunt's eyes.

"We," Aunt Jo motioned to the other family members around the fire pit, "think this would be an excellent time to have a naming ceremony for you. If the children embrace this culture, we can do one for them next year."

Shandra studied the group of women she'd become better acquainted with over the last few years. "Naming? As in a Nez Perce name?" Her heart expanded realizing this would be the ultimate rebirth of her into this side of her family.

"Of course! What other name would we give you?" Aunt Jo asked.

"Maybe, Slow to Find Her Roots," Jackie said, and they all laughed.

The joking and family camaraderie had been the first thing Shandra had noticed about her family when she'd reunited with them after nearly twenty years of no contact.

"I would be proud to have a new name. How do I get it?" She glanced around the circle of women.

"We already have it picked out. But we feel you might like to go on a vision quest." Aunt Jo glanced around at all the other women. They all nodded.

"What is a vision quest?" Shandra had read a little bit about the coming-of-age quest of Nez Perce children. As an adult she wasn't sure it was really needed, but wanted to fully embrace this whole experience.

"It is a time for you to meet up with your wyakin or guardian spirit. Andy will take you to our place, saddle up a horse, and you will ride to the highest point on our property. Your wyakin will come to you. It will guide you to your future. When you come back, you will sing about your encounter at the naming ceremony." Aunt Jo nodded as if that was all there was to it.

"But how do I know it will be my wyakin?" Nerves skittered up her spine. What if nothing came to her? Did that mean she wasn't chosen to be a member of the Nimiipuu?

"Your grandmother comes to you in dreams. I have a feeling you will have no problem speaking to your wyakin," Velma, a cousin of Aunt Jo's, said. She had helped Shandra discover the truth when Coop was a murder suspect. She also knew about Shandra's grandmother visiting her dreams.

"When will I do this? I don't want to miss anything." Shandra was excited and nervous. "What about Ryan and the twins?"

"We'll take care of them. You can go tomorrow. There won't be that much happening here until more toward the weekend." Jo handed her ears of corn. "Shuck those and we'll have dinner ready in thirty minutes."

~*~

Ryan sat on a hard round of wood mostly listening to Shandra's uncles and older cousins talk about this year's hunting trips, fishing, and the state of the government involvement in the reservation. He glanced over at his wife, talking with her family. He grinned. She'd been looking for this family inclusion her whole life. He was happy she'd finally found it.

"What do you think, Ryan?" Martin asked, drawing Ryan from his thoughts.

"Huh? About what?"

The men all laughed. "You have it bad. You can't even look away from your woman," one of Shandra's cousins said.

"Sorry. I'm happy she's so happy. She has wanted to become closer with all of you for so long that I can't help but watch her enjoy herself." He nodded toward the women.

"Do you think mom told her yet?" Andy asked his father.

"Told her what?" Ryan studied Martin Elwood,

19

Shandra's uncle.

"We're doing a naming ceremony for Shandra."

Ryan peered at each man present as they nodded their heads. "Really? That must be why she's beaming." His heart squeezed with gratitude to this family who had taken his wife in even though she'd been torn from them so many years before.

"And tomorrow, I'll take her to the ranch so she can start her vision quest." Andy nodded.

Ryan's neck cracked; his head spun so fast toward the young man. "What are you talking about?"

Martin took up the explanation. "She'll go to the highest point on our property and talk to her wyakin. Then she'll come back here and sing about the meeting and she will be named."

Ryan shook his head. "You can't send her out alone."

"She won't be alone. She'll have her wyakin to protect her." Martin glanced at the other men.

They all nodded and grinned.

"I don't like it." Ryan's head started spinning all kinds of accidents his wife could encounter out alone on the reservation. She always seemed to get herself mixed up in murders and circumstances that could get her hurt. This seemed like another one of the same.

"She'll be fine. Everyone will be here, at the powwow. Nothing can happen to her," her Uncle Timothy said.

"You don't know Shandra. She finds trouble where you least expect it."

Laughter erupted.

"No, you don't understand."

"We do understand. All women find trouble. It's in

their nature." One of Shandra's great uncles said, and stood. "I smell food. Let's see if the women fixed anything worth eating."

The others laughed and rose, walking over to the fire ring.

Ryan stood and stared at his wife, laughing with her cousins and having a good time. Would she be able to stay out of trouble?

Chapter Three

Darkness circled the powwow grounds as Shandra and Ryan strolled along the edge of the teepees and tents, talking.

"Shandra, I know how much you've dreamed of this sort of thing coming true, but going out by yourself isn't a good idea. There could be wild animals and unsavory people you'll run into."

"My safety isn't an issue. I'll be on Higheagle land. Everyone will be here. And my wyakin will protect me." Shandra stopped, grasping her husband's hands and staring up into his shadowed face. She had to make him understand how important this act was, not only in her life, but the life of every Nimiipuu who came before and would come after her. It was their spiritual well-being that was enhanced by the vision quest as well as their feeling more a part of their culture, and in her case, family.

"This is a great honor. I never dreamed this would

be something I would participate in one day. You can not like it, but I will be going with Andy tomorrow and I will come back having met my guardian spirit, knowing my future, and then at the naming ceremony, I will fully be welcomed into my family and heritage."

Ryan drew his hands from hers and wrapped his arms around her. "You know we, you and I, are never safe. We've ferreted out many murderers, and I'm still not sure if the people I ratted out as an undercover cop have forgotten me. For those reasons, I don't like you going secluded places alone."

She understood his concerns, but this was her life and a culture she had been yearning to be included in her whole life. She kissed his chin. "I will be careful." As much as she wanted this quest to be as authentic as possible, she planned to take her phone in case she did get into trouble. She was wise enough to not go up a mountain alone without one. Whether she could get a signal… that was another thing.

"Come on. I need some sleep if I'm going to meet my wyakin tomorrow." She linked her arm in his and headed back toward her family's pod of tents and teepees.

A sound to her right drew her attention. A shadow darted between tents. She stopped and stared.

"What?" Ryan whispered in her ear.

"Someone was running between the tents." She pointed the direction she'd seen the shadow. At that moment, the person stopped, looked back, and then took off faster. A shiver traveled down her spine.

Ryan started to move away from her.

"No. Stay." She linked her arm tighter around his. "He saw me pointing."

"Come on." Ryan grasped Shandra's hand and started back toward the Higheagle camp at just under a jog. He should have known. Not only was she determined to go off alone on a mountain tomorrow, but now someone who was lurking in the shadows of the tents knew she'd seen him.

He didn't take her to their teepee, he walked up to the fire where several of the men in her family were still sitting around B.S.ing. "I don't think this trip you want Shandra to take tomorrow is a good idea."

"Ryan! I told you. I'm going. You are only going to make this week miserable for all of us if you continue to be stubborn about it." Shandra stared at him. He could see she was determined, but whatever she saw among the tents had also shaken her.

He sighed. "Is there a way to make sure she is safe? She just saw someone lurking around the tents by the vendors."

"You sure it wasn't just a young buck teepee creeping?" Uncle Timothy said, and the others all laughed.

"No," Shandra said, shaking her head. "I couldn't see his face, but when he looked at me, pointing him out to Ryan, I felt…" she shuddered. "He was up to no good."

Uncle Martin stood. "Where did you see this?"

"You go in with the kids. I'll take your uncle to the place." Ryan led Shandra to their teepee and held the flap as she entered. He returned to Martin and her uncle Lloyd. "Shandra feels things—"

Martin held up a hand. "You don't need to tell us about her abilities. We all know. Show us where you were."

Ryan nodded and backtracked to the spot where Shandra had seen the man. He pointed as she had. "In there. I barely saw him move. He was headed straight across the pod."

"This is not a family pod. It is for the people who come from other places to sell their goods. It could have been someone we don't know." Martin peered at the group of tents.

"If someone was lurking around these tents it is a good thing to think they were finding a way to steal," Uncle Lloyd said.

"But they haven't set up and sold anything yet. There would be more money later in the week." Martin faced Lloyd.

"Then he was casing the tents. Figuring out who would be the best ones to steal from." Ryan knew all about this from his time spent policing in Chicago. "It might be a good idea to tell the vendors to be extra careful." He turned and walked back toward the Higheagle camp.

The two men followed, jabbering about how it would be an affront to the powwow to have someone rob the vendors.

Ryan entered the teepee. Shandra was in her pajamas but sitting up in their makeshift bed. A flashlight sat beside the bed, shining light up toward the hole in the top of the structure.

"What did you find?" she whispered.

He slipped out of his clothes and down to his underwear before sliding into the sleeping bag with her. "Martin and Lloyd think it might have been someone figuring out who of the vendors would be the best to steal from."

"No!" she whispered loudly. "Here? Someone would steal from the vendors?"

"They said it's never happened but that doesn't keep it from being on a desperate person's mind." He kissed her. "Go to sleep. You have a big day tomorrow."

A smile tipped her lips. "I do."

~*~

Shandra sat atop one of the Higheagle's best appaloosa geldings.

"Just keep heading for the top of that hill. It's the highest spot on our property. Sit and wait for your wyakin to show up." Andy pointed to the hill where she'd found Coop hiding out when he was a murder suspect.

"Okay. What if my wyakin doesn't show up?" Even though her aunt was positive she wouldn't have to wait long for her wyakin given Ella visited her in dreams, Shandra was skeptical her guardian spirit would show itself considering how many years she'd spent not caring about her culture.

"You stay until it shows. It took me two days—"

"Two days! Do you know how worried Ryan would be if I didn't come back for two days?" Her husband would call the search and rescue if she didn't return tonight.

"When you come back down, go in the house, call me, and then get something to drink and eat. You can't have water or food when you are seeking your wyakin." Andy walked toward his pickup. "Enjoy the experience."

Shandra smiled at her cousin, but inside her stomach was clenching and unclenching. What if her wyakin didn't come to her?

~*~

After Aunt Jo sent the twins and Fawn off to play with their cousins, Ryan decided he needed to make himself useful. It was that or worry about Shandra.

"Come on. There is work that needs done to prepare for the events," Martin said, dumping the last of his coffee into their dead campfire and standing.

"Sounds good." Ryan rose off his log seat as a scream ricocheted through the tents and teepees.

"Which direction did that come from?" Martin asked.

Ryan had a vague idea but the running people, was a good indication. "That way."

They both ran with the others to the tents where the vendors were setting up. A young woman stood in front of one of the tents, her face covered by her hands.

Ryan slowed and studied all the people standing around the woman. They were all ages and most had sympathetic expressions. Except one woman who appeared to be in her sixties. She had a smug smile. A young man moved through the crowd and consoled the younger woman.

"What's going on here?" A man with two long, gray, thin braids flapping on the breast pockets of the western shirt he wore, marched up to the group.

The young man shifted his attention from the woman to the older man. "Millie said grandmother is dead."

Ryan shoved through the group. "Where?"

The young woman pointed toward the tent behind her.

He pushed through the opening and spotted the

older woman they'd witnessed being threatened yesterday, on her back, a colorful beaded necklace tightly wrapped around her neck.

The sound of someone entering behind him, had Ryan spinning around. It was Martin. "Keep everyone out of here and call the local police. This woman was murdered." He scanned the inside of the tent for sign of a struggle.

Martin said something in the language Ryan had learned was Sahaptin, the language of the tribes in Oregon, Washington, and Idaho, and exited the tent.

Ryan pulled out his phone and took photos as if it was his crime scene. He had no jurisdiction here, but he might be of some help to the reservation police. If Officer Logan Rider came, it would make his intrusion on their homicide easier. He'd worked with the man before when Coop was a murder suspect and Fawn's mother was murdered right before his and Shandra's wedding.

He found the cash box in a tote with what appeared to be beaded necklaces a lot like the one around the woman's neck. He remembered Aunt Jo saying this woman made wonderful beadwork that Shandra should see. That sent his mind to his wife and wondering how she was doing out in the hot July sun waiting for a guardian spirit to find her.

~*~

Shandra rode the gelding, Swift, to the top of the hill. There were two trees near the top but nothing at the very top. Since she was the one seeking her wyakin and not the horse, she tied him to one of the trees where he could nibble the grass and hide in the shade.

Finding a somewhat grassy spot, if there was such

a thing on the top of a hill that was buffeted by wind and baked by sun, Shandra sat down, closed her eyes, and waited.

The sun beat down on her, trickling sweat down the sides of her face and between her breasts. Opening her eyes, she focused on the trees and pretended she was in the shade.

As her body cooled, thinking about the rustle of leaves and a cool breeze, she drifted off to the shade. She lay on her back, relaxing, dreaming of the next vase she'd like to make. The vision of the vase took shape in the limbs of the tree above her. When the vase was complete, it shattered and a silver wolf dropped to the ground beside her.

Shandra startled, sitting up, waiting for the wolf to growl and snap. Instead, the animal's amber eyes peered into hers and she heard a voice. "*Keep your cubs close, help them grow, teach them how to survive.*"

The image vanished, the heat baked her back, and Shandra opened her hand. A tuft of silver hair lay in her palm.

She scanned the hillside. The only animal in sight was Swift and a rabbit hopping out from under a sagebrush. If not for the fur in her hand, she would have thought the whole event was a dream brought on from heat exhaustion.

The wolf had to have been her wyakin. What did it all mean?

Chapter Four

After taking as many photos as he could and looking around without touching anything, Ryan stepped out of the tent as two Tribal Police Officers walked through the crowd still standing around.

Officer Rider held out his hand and smiled. "Detective Greer. Good to see you. Is your wife around?"

"She's off waiting for her guardian spirit. Glad to see you caught this." Ryan led the two officers into the tent.

"Poor Lucille," Officer Rider said, standing over the body. "Sam, start taking photos."

The other, younger officer, pulled out a compact camera and circled the body taking the same photos Ryan had.

"Who is she?" he asked, looking away from her bulging eyes and blue lips.

"Lucille Lightning. She is well known for her

beadwork." Logan shook his head. "She has been teaching classes at the center to the young people. Beading, the kind Lucille does-did, is an art that will soon vanish if we don't share it with our youth."

"Would she have more money in here than the other vendors?" While Ryan was pretty sure she hadn't come upon someone stealing her money, he had to ask.

"Her work is worth more than the others, but I doubt she had much more in here right now than any of the other vendors." Logan faced him. "She did call in one night asking about a thing she'd heard about called a restraining order."

Ryan focused on the officer. "Who did she want it against?"

"Scott, her grandson," the other officer, Sam, said.

Watching the younger officer continue taking photos, Ryan asked, "What do you know about Scott?"

"We went to school together. He has wanted his grandmother's place since high school."

"Won't he get it? I mean, wouldn't he have gotten it eventually?" Ryan didn't understand how a grandchild could kill the reason they were alive.

"There are only the two grandchildren and an aunt. I believe the land would have gone to all of them and Scott would have had to buy the others out." Sam stopped taking photos and stared at Ryan. "Word around here is she was unhappy with Scott and Marian, his wife, and was talking about leaving everything to Millie."

Ryan's gaze shot to the tent opening. "The young woman who found the body."

Logan strode to the tent opening and stepped out. Ryan followed.

"Millie, Scott…" Logan scanned the rest of the crowd. "Is Marian around?"

"She's at home taking care of the horses," Scott said.

"You two, over to the side of the tent. The rest of you go about your business." Logan stood with his arms folded across his chest, his round boyish face and smile relieving some of the worry Ryan felt as they'd stepped out of the tent.

The group slowly dispersed. Uncle Martin glanced at Ryan. He nodded and the man walked away.

Ryan joined Logan and the siblings.

"When was the last time either of you saw Lucille alive?" Logan asked, his logbook open and pen poised.

"I was at home all day yesterday. We had a colicky horse," Scott said.

Ryan cleared his throat.

Logan glanced at him. "You think differently?"

"He looks a lot like the guy we saw arguing with the victim yesterday afternoon." Ryan stared at the young man.

Logan focused on the grandson. "Were you arguing with your grandmother yesterday?"

The man rubbed a hand over his face, his lips pressed together.

"Did you argue with her again?" the young woman, Millie asked, hitting her brother's arm. "You know she hasn't been feeling well. How could you?"

"What's been wrong with her?" Logan asked as if he hadn't seen the beads wrapped around the woman's swollen neck.

"She had a physical last week after a dizzy spell. The doctor said she had high blood pressure and needed to not do things that caused stress." The woman stared at her brother.

"Hey! I wasn't the only one she had trouble with. Morton was chewing on her when I walked up."

"But you knew about her high blood pressure! Why would you argue with her after she and Morton had one of their rounds?" The young woman threw her hands in the air, walked away, and returned. "Do you think she had a heart attack?" She studied Logan as she asked.

"Millie, I'm pretty sure when the body is examined it will show she was murdered."

"No!" She glared at her brother. "You mean someone killed her?"

Ryan knew it was best to keep the matter of how she died quiet. "Yes, that's what it looks like. Can you think of anyone else who might have wanted your grandmother dead?"

"You mean besides me? I see the way you look at me. I wouldn't kill my grandmother. We had differences, but…" the young man's eyes teared up and he swiped at them.

"I can't think of anyone. She was happy, loved working with beads and teaching others." Millie's shoulders slumped. "Who will teach the rest of us this art?"

"You two may go. Are you staying at the powwow grounds?" Logan asked.

"I am at our mother's family camp." Millie glanced at the tent. "Will I still be able to sell Grandmother's beadwork? She had asked me to help her this year."

"It will depend on whether or not that is evidence." Logan put a hand on her shoulder and squeezed. "I'll let you know what I find out."

Millie nodded and walked away, her head bowed.

"From what you said, I take it you aren't staying here?" Logan asked.

Ryan didn't miss the quick flick of Scott's gaze the direction his sister had walked.

"I'm not staying here. Marian needs help with the horses." He shrugged. "Can I go home now?"

"As long as you stay there or here, so I can find you if I have more questions." Logan glanced at Ryan. "You have anything you want to ask him?"

"What were you and your grandmother arguing about that she wanted to get a restraining order against you?"

The young man flinched. "She really planned to go through with that?"

Logan nodded.

"It wasn't me. It was Marian. She's been bringing in horses to board and train, to help make money. Grandmother didn't like her bringing other people's problem horses to our property. Grandmother believed bad horses brought trouble." He shrugged. "Marian believes there aren't any bad horses, only people who don't know how to communicate with them."

Ryan glanced at Logan. He was nodding. And he was pretty sure, Shandra would say the same thing. "Thank you."

As Scott started walking away, Ryan called, "Where were you last night about ten?"

Logan studied Ryan. "Tell you in a minute," Ryan said as the young man spun around and stared at him.

"Why?"

"Just answer the question," Logan said, advancing

toward Scott.

"Home."

"Anyone else there?" Ryan asked.

"Marian."

Ryan and Logan exchanged glances.

"Anyone else verify that?" Ryan asked.

"No. What is this?" Scott walked back toward them.

"I saw someone sneaking between these tents last night around ten." Ryan faced Logan. "I'll tell you more as we finish up in the tent."

~*~

Shandra remained sitting on top of the hill admiring the warmth of the sun, the scent of sagebrush on the breeze blowing by, and the beauty she'd just witnessed in her wyakin. Aunt Jo said she was to sing about her encounter. It was still as surreal to her as the fact her grandmother came to her in dreams. She knew it happened. Her hand still held several hairs from touching the wolf. That she heard the animal speak to her in her mind, she shook her head. How was that possible?

A cloud floated by, shielding the sun's July rays and reminding Shandra she should head down the hill and call Andy to pick her up. Ryan would be worried if she stayed up here until dark. Though darkness didn't come until nearly ten o-clock this time of year.

She stood, glanced the direction the wolf had headed after their encounter, and smiled. One day, she hoped they'd meet again.

Chapter Five

"Hey, Shandra just called. I'm going to pick her up," Andy said, jogging by where Ryan stood with Logan, a Washington State Trooper, and the coroner who had arrived last at around two.

"Did she say if she…" Ryan wasn't sure how many people were supposed to know why Shandra was gone.

"She did. I could tell by her voice. See you in an hour or so." Andy disappeared.

Logan raised an eyebrow. "Are you ready for the naming ceremony?"

Ryan shrugged. "I haven't been ready for anything since meeting Shandra."

The tribal officer laughed and slapped him on the back. "I wondered about that the first time I met her."

"Here's the paperwork. Have the body sent to Spokane, I'll get on the autopsy as soon as it arrives." The coroner handed Logan and the State Trooper several papers and walked back to his vehicle.

"How long until the body is picked up?" Ryan asked.

Logan shrugged. "Depends on which funeral home is called to transport it to Spokane."

"Someone has to stay with the body until it's hauled off."

"Forensics are still gathering evidence," the trooper said. "When they finish, the scene can be cleared."

"I'll stick around until then." Logan stood by the door of the tent watching everyone who wandered by.

"This isn't my jurisdiction. I'll just head back to the Higheagle camp. Come get me if you need any help." Ryan pointed the toes of his cowboy boots toward the half a dozen tents and teepees housing Shandra's family and theirs.

"I'll keep that in mind." Logan grinned.

Ryan wasn't sure if the man was joking with him or would come to him if he needed help. He waved and strode over to the fire where Shandra's aunts and cousins were preparing the evening meal.

He grabbed a piece of firewood and sat down next to Aunt Jo. "Tell me everything you know about Lucille Lightning."

"She's nearly fifteen years older than me. She has always been an influence in getting the younger people interested in our culture. Language, beading, dance. She traveled to many powwows on the west coast."

Ryan nodded. "Tell me about her family."

Aunt Jo stared into his eyes. "You can't think her family had anything to do with her death?"

"It helps to find out who wanted her dead by understanding the family." He hoped Jo didn't balk at telling him everything. All the sordid details of the

37

Lightning family members.

"She had two boys and a girl. One son died as a teenager in a car accident. The other was in the military. He killed himself five years ago. That's when Scott and Millie went to live with their grandmother. Their mother couldn't deal with them. Lucille's daughter married off the reservation and hasn't been back."

"Then the only close family she had are the brother and sister? Her grandchildren?" Ryan didn't see why the grandson would need to kill the grandmother to get the land. He would have been in line to inherit. Maybe she wasn't dying soon enough for him—or his wife.

"Yes. Her husband passed nearly twenty years ago." Jo stood, stirred whatever was in the large pot, and sat back down.

"The grandchildren would have inherited her land whenever she passed?" he asked, glancing around at the other women present.

Aunt Velma cleared her throat. "Usually the land and belongings pass down to the next living relative. Since Geri hasn't been seen in these parts in thirty years, it would most likely go to Scott and Millie."

"There wouldn't be a reason for them to want their grandmother dead to get the land then." Ryan glanced around the ring of women. Their faces were all fixed in the same non-committal stony face. "What did I say?"

"We can't believe Scott and Millie would kill Lucille. She took them in and cared for them when they didn't have anyone else." Jo stood. "Perhaps you should take this conversation over to the men."

Ryan shook his head. Women knew the most about the community around them. "Who besides someone named Morton have you heard or seen Lucille having problems with?"

"Morton Yellowtail? He's always telling Lucille she tries too hard to get the youth interested in the old ways. He feels we would be better to have more computers in the center and less classes on basket weaving, beading, and language." Jo became animated. "He should not be on the center's board. He wants everything to be like a center for youth off the reservation. He doesn't care about our culture."

"I see. Was there anything in particular he was trying to get across to Lucille lately? Something that she was holding him up from getting?" Ryan wasn't sure the method of murder was a crime of passion, but neither did he think it was pre-meditated. The body, method of strangulation, and nothing stolen had him at a loss for who or why the poor woman was killed.

"Her vote was holding up money to be issued for three new computers," Jo said. "But I don't see Morton killing Lucille for that."

"The only person I can think of that would want Lucille out of the way is Kitty," Velma stood up, hitched up her pants on her six-foot frame and squared her wide shoulders. "She has been moaning that Lucille's work is getting inferior due to her age and she should stop making jewelry that reflects badly on the rest of them." Velma snorted very unlady-like. "It's the other way around. Kitty's work is inferior and once someone sees what Lucille has made, they realize it."

"Competition then." He liked the idea of someone who made jewelry using the woman's own necklace to kill her. "How old is Kitty?"

"She's my age," Jo said.

Ryan stood. "Could one of you introduce me to

her?"

Velma nodded. "I'd like to do that."

"Velma, be nice," Jo reprimanded the woman.

Ryan had heard from Shandra how her Aunt Velma could be pushy and brash and most of the Nespelem community was scared of her. Now was his chance to see it in action from the stride the woman was taking them out of the Higheagle camp and over to the vendor tents.

~*~

Andy pulled up to the house. Shandra sat on the back-porch steps. She'd unsaddled the horse and put him up after calling Andy for a ride back to the powwow grounds.

"Thanks for coming so quick," she said, sliding into the passenger side of her cousin's pickup.

"No problem. Your husband caught a murder while you were gone."

"He what?" Shandra stared at Andy. "Who was murdered?"

"Lucille Lightning."

"The woman we saw arguing with a young man yesterday?"

"Her grandson. Yep." Andy pulled out of the ranch and onto the county road.

"How?"

"I don't know. Ryan and Logan aren't saying much."

She nodded. "They don't want to give too much away. It's how they catch the person up who did it." She'd helped her husband solve enough murders the last few years to know how the whole process worked. "I'm glad Logan is on this. Any idea why she was killed?"

Andy shook his head. "Not a clue. She was a nice lady. Taught the youth skills that are getting lost." He went on to tell her about the classes she taught at the center and how she made a living off her beadwork and baskets.

"She must have traveled from powwow to powwow," Shandra said out loud.

"Yeah. That and her granddaughter, Millie, set up a website that sells her grandmother's beadwork and baskets."

Shandra had seen the glow that was in Andy's eyes before. Only then it was his older brother talking about the woman he'd eventually married. "Tell me about Millie."

A smile crept across Andy's face before he said, "She's smarter than anyone I know. She's cute but doesn't know it. Devoted to her grandmother. And she doesn't mind that I already have a daughter." His voice trailed off and his round face drooped. "I need to check on her when we get back to the grounds."

"Is she staying there with family?" Shandra asked.

"Her mom's side. Her dad was Lucille's oldest son. He came back from Afghanistan and never was the same. At least that's what Millie said. He killed himself five years ago. His wife had used Lucille and her parents to take care of the kids when her husband was gone in the military. After he died, Lucille suggested Scott and Millie live with her. Then Scott married Marian and she moved in." He shook his head. "Lucille and Marian didn't get along. Marian didn't want anything to do with beadwork or basket making. She has always cared only for horses." He glanced over at

41

Shandra. "Honestly, I think she only married Scott knowing he'd one day own Lucille's land. It is not far from Nespelem to the west, handy for people to bring her horses to train and has a good barn and corrals."

"Then you know her well because of your horse breeding." Shandra studied her cousin. He didn't seem to care for the woman who would now own Lucille's property with her husband.

"Yeah. I can tell you this. I wouldn't take any of my horses to her to train. The ones I've seen act as if someone has beaten them into submission. That isn't the way to train a horse. They'll turn on you one day."

Shandra had to agree with his thoughts. If you treated an animal, or a person poorly, they could turn on you.

~*~

Velma led Ryan to a tent much like the one where the homicide was committed. She shook the canvas. "Kitty, come out so we can talk!"

Ryan stared at the way Velma's nostrils flared and the set of her chin. He wouldn't doubt, if Kitty didn't walk out, Velma would go into the tent and drag her out.

A small woman in her sixties stepped out of the tent. She didn't have a pleased expression but she was the same woman Ryan had noticed at the crime scene tent. The smug smile was replaced with distaste.

"What do you want, Velma?" the woman asked. The glare in her eyes softened at the sight of Ryan. "Who are you? You were awful friendly with Logan Rider."

"He's married to my niece," Velma said. "We were wondering if you had any arguments with Lucille lately." The larger woman loomed over the smaller one.

Ryan stepped between them, making them both move backwards. "I heard you and Lucille had some disagreements. What were they about?"

"Why are you asking?"

He'd had his share of belligerent interviewees. "I'm trying to help Officer Rider with his investigation. If you can tell me your relationship with the deceased, I can relay that information to him and save him time coming to see you."

She laughed. "I don't have anything to tell anyone."

Velma stepped around him. "In other words, you probably killed Lucille."

Kitty huffed some words Ryan didn't know, pivoted, and ducked into the tent.

Velma didn't intimidate this woman, but she'd definitely pissed her off.

Chapter Six

By the smells emanating from the campground and the growling of her stomach, Shandra could tell they'd arrived in time for dinner. She stepped out of Andy's pickup and two small arms wrapped around her waist.

"Mia, what are you doing out here in the parking area?" Shandra's body tensed worrying someone was chasing her daughter.

"We saw Andy drive in over there." She pointed toward the entrance to the grounds. "I ran over here because I wanted to show you something."

Shandra hugged the girl and took hold of one of her hands. "Do we have time before dinner?"

Mia nodded. "Aunt Jo said, there would be time to show you. Come on. They're in our teepee."

"They? Is someone waiting for us?" She couldn't think of anyone she hadn't talked with already. Other than Coop and Sandy. But they wouldn't arrive for another two days.

44

Mia laughed. "No. You'll see." She stopped in front of the teepee, released Shandra's hand, and grasped the edge of the flap. "Go see."

Shandra smiled at the excitement on Mia's face and stepped into the teepee. Hanging from one of the poles were matching jingle dresses. One for an adult and one for a child Mia's size. They had the same beaded pattern on the hats, but the colors were different.

"Where?" Shandra walked forward and touched the bright colored fabric.

"Aunt Jo made them for us. She said she knew one day we would come to the powwow and need to dance the healing dance." Mia's face scrunched up. "Did you know the Jingle Dance is a healing dance?"

She did, but she pretended not to know.

"Aunt Jo said because of the loss in our lives it would do us both good to dance." Mia touched the smaller dress. "She said I was to let the dance heal me." She glanced up at Shandra. "I didn't know I was sick."

Shandra pulled the child into an embrace. "You aren't sick, like a sour tummy or a cold. She means, because you lost your mom, dad, and aunt and how they were taken from you, your heart needs to heal."

She could tell Mia still didn't understand, but then what eight-year-old understood the harshness that they had endured when they had known nothing else.

Her stomach growled.

"Come on. Aunt Jo said we had to get you to dinner because you haven't eaten all day." Mia grasped her hands and stared into her face. "Why didn't you eat? I know Andy took you to a hill but I don't understand the rest."

"I'll tell you, Jayden, and Ryan all about it after dinner. Though I can't tell you everything. It's a secret I have to sing to everyone one night this week." She still wasn't sure how to do that, but planned to ask her aunt for help.

"There you are," Ryan stepped into the teepee, his gaze latching onto Shandra's.

"Mia wanted to show me our jingle dresses." Shandra stepped forward and used her free hand to capture one of Ryan's. He squeezed her hand, and she reciprocated the action.

"They are works of art. Your aunt put a lot of hours into those dresses." Ryan led them both out of the teepee.

"I agree." Shandra released Mia's hand. "Run ahead and tell Aunt Jo we're coming."

"Okay." The child took off at a run toward the table holding the camp stoves where Aunt Jo and Velma stood.

"Did you learn anything about how Lucille Lightning was killed?"

Ryan stopped and studied her. "How did you know—. Your grandmother came to you up on the hill?"

She laughed. "No. Andy told me about it on the drive back." She frowned. It had upset her that Ella hadn't come to her while she sat waiting for her wyakin.

"Did you see whatever it was you were supposed to see?" Ryan peered into her eyes.

"Yes. It was…There is nothing that can describe it." She placed a hand on the pant pocket that held the fur. She'd ask Aunt Jo what she was to do with it. She knew it had to have a significance for her to have ended up with the fur in her hand.

Ryan put an arm across her shoulders. "Let's eat. You have to be hungry."

"I am."

Walking into the family circle, she felt all eyes on her. By the smiles and bobbing heads, she knew Andy had told everyone her wyakin had come to her.

"You get the first plate," Aunt Jo said, stepping forward with a plate piled with stew and fry bread.

"Thank you." Shandra noticed there were more family members than the night before, more tents and teepees, and tonight there were folding chairs and tables to sit and eat. She took a spot where she could watch everyone and sat. She was on her fifth bite of the delicious stew when Ryan and the twins placed their plates along her side of the table.

Jayden started talking animatedly about his day. Shandra listened and smiled, enjoying the boy's enthusiasm and excitement.

"That sounds like a great day," she said.

"And Billy helped me put my stuff in the boy's tent," he said.

Ryan laughed. "I don't think the men sleeping in the tent would like to hear you call it a boy's tent."

"What about the boy's tent?" Andy asked, as he and Fawn sat in the chairs across the table from them.

"Ryan thinks you'd be mad hearing me call the tent we sleep in the boy's tent." Jayden stared at his older cousin. "Are you? Mad?"

"No. I like sleeping in the boy's tent. I get to know my cousins better." Andy reached over and tapped his fork against Jayden's as if they were making a pact.

Jayden beamed. "See, he likes it."

Mia made a noise, and Shandra looked down at the child. Her bottom lip stuck out in a pout. "What's wrong?"

"I want to sleep in a girl's tent."

"Girls sleep with their parents to learn how to take care of their family." Andy said this and then his gaze darted to a group of people at the end of the table. He stood. "Millie, over here."

"What's Millie doing at our camp?" Shandra asked in a low voice.

"I invited her." Andy grinned, stood, and then introduced the young woman who walked over. She sat on the other side of Fawn.

Ryan bumped Shandra's leg under the table. She glanced at him before leaning close for him to whisper, "She's a suspect."

Shandra shook her head and whispered back, "Andy is in love with her."

Ryan narrowed his eyes. "It doesn't change anything."

"Change what?" Andy asked.

"Nothing," Shandra said, to stop her husband from stating what he'd just told her.

Millie glanced up from her plate. Her gaze landed on Ryan. "You're the cop who was with Logan at Grandmother's tent. Can I go in and see if anything is missing?"

Ryan felt his wife's hand squeezing his leg. He wasn't sure what that was meant to mean, but he opened his mouth and said, "You'll have to ask Logan. I don't have any jurisdiction here."

"What do you think was taken?" Shandra asked.

He should have known she wouldn't stay out of this murder any more than she had all the others they'd encountered since their first meeting.

"If the money wasn't…" Millie studied Ryan.

He acquiesced. "How much did she have?"

"Maybe a couple hundred in small bills."

"Then I don't think money was taken. Anyway, the cash box looked untouched." Ryan leaned forward. "What else do you think would have been taken?"

Millie leaned forward, glanced at the children, pressed a finger to her lips as if telling Mia, Jayden, and Fawn to not say a word and then said in a soft voice, "Grandmother had a new design she was working on for a catalog client, and she had just purchased three stones that are known for their healing powers."

Shandra leaned toward Millie. "Why would the new design be stolen?"

"Grandmother was picked from many who showed their work to this catalog. They picked Grandmother and asked her to come up with a new design, like what she already did, but different. If someone found it and offered it to the company now that Grandmother isn't alive, they could get the contract." Millie glanced at Andy. "If I can find the design, I can make the bracelet, necklace, and earrings to keep the contract. I could continue the Lightning Beadwork."

Ryan knew what his wife was thinking the minute she spun his direction.

"You should call Logan and see if you can escort Millie to the tent to look for those items." Shandra peered into his eyes.

"I am here on vacation. This isn't my jurisdiction." He stated, peering at each of the adults at their end of the table.

"But you are just as curious about all of this as anyone else." Shandra bumped his shoulder with hers. "Maybe more."

Andy handed Ryan his phone. "I have Logan's number on my phone."

Ryan waved his hand. "I have it. Excuse me." He stood and walked away from all the people sitting about eating their dinner.

Scrolling through the names, he found Logan Rider and hit the button to call. He knew when he'd been one of the first on the scene, he wouldn't be able to stay out of the investigation during his stay here. However, he had hoped to keep Shandra and the kids out of it. He should have known better.

"Rider, speak your piece," boomed the tribal police officer's voice.

"Hey, Logan, it's Ryan Greer. Millie said there could have been other things besides money the person was looking for in the victim's tent. Do you want to wait and have her go through it with you or can I take her in and let her look?"

The man laughed. "I can tell by the excitement in your voice, your wife put you up to this. *Ays*?"

Ryan had learned from his first trip to the reservation the people who lived here enjoyed a good joke. Luckily, they always added the *ays* on the end of a joke. Otherwise there were times when he wasn't sure if it was a slur on him if not for that one word.

"Funny. And yeah, she did. But if the items Millie is talking about are as important as she says, they could have been worth killing for."

"I'm off duty and could swing by. My grandmother

has been giving me hell about not stopping in unofficially. Can you wait about thirty minutes? I'll let Grandmother know I'm there and then meet you and Millie at the tent."

"Copy." Ryan walked back to the tables. Many of the family members had finished and were milling around in small groups. Jayden had left. Mia sat beside Shandra telling her about her day.

He walked up to Andy and Millie who were talking softly among themselves. "Logan will be here in thirty minutes. He said we were to meet him at the tent then."

Andy glanced at his watch. "Okay."

Ryan picked up Shandra and Mia's empty plates and carried them over to a large garbage sack already bulging from paper plates, napkins, and cups.

"Have you had a chance to talk to Shandra about today?" Aunt Jo asked.

"No. Mia has been keeping her occupied. Why?" He studied the woman.

"I just wondered if she'd said anything about her wyakin." The woman seemed interested but also as if she were watching for him to do something wrong.

"She didn't say anything. We haven't had time to talk." He raised an eyebrow.

"She isn't to tell anyone, not even you, about the experience today. She must keep it to herself and only sing of it before the naming ceremony."

"How do you know what to name her if you don't know anything about her experience until she sings. And by the way, she is not a very good singer." If he'd said that in front of Shandra she would have had a comeback about his singing ability.

Jo shook her head. "Just make sure she doesn't tell

anyone." She walked away.

Ryan glanced over at the table. Shandra and Mia were standing.

Chapter Seven

Shandra wanted to go with Ryan to the tent where Lucille Lightning had died. She wanted to see the woman's work and get a feel for who could have wanted her dead. After taking Mia to her cousin Jackie's teepee to play with her girls, Shandra hurried over to the area where she'd seen the person the night before.

It was still light, though the sun was slowly lowering, throwing short stumpy shadows. Wondering if the person she'd seen the night before had been coming or going to Lucille's tent, she walked out to the edge where she and Ryan had been and looked in. It was easy to see where the murder had happened. The tent had crime scene tape all around it and a tribal policeman sat on a chair in front of it.

Her line of sight from this spot to the tent, meant the person she'd seen, could have been the killer. If only she could remember more about them. She wasn't sure if it was a man or a woman. They had been in black clothing, with a hood pulled over their head.

Ryan, Logan, Andy, and Millie walked up to the tent.

Shandra wove her way around the other vendor tents, joining them.

"What are you doing here?" Ryan asked, pulling her to the side.

"I want to see Lucille's work and watch Millie's reactions," Shandra whispered.

"No. Go back to the camp. You may have seen the killer last night and they saw you. I want you to remain around family members." Ryan glanced over her shoulder. "I need to go in."

"So do I. Remaining with you is safer if you think the killer will come after me." She didn't think the killer would. She had no idea who it was and would make sure everyone knew that. But she did want to watch Millie. As much for the sake of the murder, as for Andy.

Ryan sighed. "Don't touch anything."

Shandra ducked around him. "I know."

Her first impressions of the inside of the tent were the smell and the closeness. An earthy combination of herbs and the smell she'd come to associate with death. Five people in the space with stacked boxes, folded tables, Indian blankets, and what looked like the woman's bed made the inside crowded.

"Andy, you and Shandra step outside so Millie can move around and look," Logan said.

Andy grabbed Shandra by the arm. "Come on. Let's give them room."

Ryan added, "You saw, now go. Andy, stay with

her."

Her cousin glanced at Ryan, nodded, and drew her out of the tent.

"I wanted to watch Millie go through the things," she said to Andy when they stepped outside.

"She didn't kill her grandmother." Andy crossed his arms and stared at her.

"But she may recognize something, or have an idea when she looks at something. If she keeps it to herself, she could…" Shandra didn't finish the sentence as an elderly man walked up to them.

"What's going on? They hauled poor Lucille out this afternoon."

"Elias, this is my cousin, Shandra. Her husband, Logan, and Millie are going through Lucille's things to see if anything is missing."

Shandra glared at Andy. He shouldn't be telling everyone what was happening in the investigation. "How did you know Lucille?" she asked to keep the man from asking questions she was certain Andy would answer.

"We've been going from powwow to powwow for the last ten years selling our goods."

"What do you make?" she asked.

"I make flutes. The original kind from elderberry stems. And some bone whistles. Me and Lucille, we stuck with the same things our ancestors made. She sure could tell a story with her beadwork." A tear appeared in his faded brown eyes. "Her work, both the beading and working with the youth, will be missed."

"Did you see anyone around here last night? After ten?" The man had stepped out of the tent right next to Lucille's.

"I thought I heard something after I'd gone to bed. Footsteps maybe. I know it wasn't a four-legged animal."

"You didn't look out to see?" The tent moved and the flap opened. Ryan stepped out, caught sight of them, and walked over.

"No. I sleep on a cot and once I get down on that thing, I don't want to get up again until morning." He glanced at Ryan. "You must be her man. Did you learn anything in there?"

"It's hard to say." Ryan touched Shandra's arm. "Logan wants you to look at something."

Shandra grinned. She should have known Logan would keep her involved in the murder. He knew about her dreams. She'd told him about them before.

"Andy, wait for Millie. I think she'd like an escort back to her family." Ryan had figured out the two were interested in one another and from what Millie had said before and while in the tent, she might have a clue to who had killed her grandmother.

Andy nodded and Ryan escorted Shandra into the tent. He didn't like involving his wife any more than she already was, but Logan felt she was more knowledgeable about art, galleries, and sales of art than anyone else at the event.

"Logan, what's up?" Shandra asked, a smug smile on her face.

Ryan wasn't sure what kind of connection his wife and the big tribal officer had but he'd witnessed it before. He thought it had something to do with their grandmothers having been best friends.

"Millie found these brochures from art galleries in Seattle and Jackson Hole. You know anything about

56

them?" Logan held the pamphlets out to Shandra.

Ryan could have used his phone and looked them up just as easily as Shandra looking at them.

"This one, in Seattle, I've met the owner at a Native American show in Tulsa. She and her husband seemed to be knowledgeable about the artists and the mediums used by Native Americans." She placed the second one on top of the other one. She tapped it with a finger. "This one, I think I heard my friends Naomi and Ted talking about them one day. I remember wondering how they could stay in business with a bad reputation. You want me to contact my friends and see what else I can find out?"

"I'll let you know. Millie says the new design Lucille was working on is missing. She saw it two days ago?" he questioned the young woman.

She nodded. "She had asked my opinion of a color choice. She still had a bit more of the design to figure out on the edge of the medallion."

"You would know it if you saw it?" Shandra asked.

"Yes. I can draw it from memory. All that I saw." Millie glanced at each person.

"That's a good idea," Logan said. "But don't tell anyone what you're doing."

"I don't understand. What difference does it make?" Millie moved to a tote, opened the lid, and pulled out a drawing pad and pencil.

"Because if the person who stole the design learns you know what it looks like, you could be the next victim," Ryan said, getting a glare from Logan and a gasp from his wife. "It's the truth. If you are going on the assumption the victim was murdered for her design, whoever knows about it will be a target. Unless it was

57

someone who stole the design and plans to use it far from here." He studied Millie. "Do you think there is anyone here who would be dumb enough to try and sell a piece of beadwork in this area with that design?"

She shook her head. "It would take hours of work. It would never be finished in time to sell at this powwow."

"But if you saw it at another powwow or in a catalog, you would recognize it and realize what had happened." Ryan motioned toward the young woman. "That would make you a target. Making it a good idea for you to keep quiet."

"You might want to tell Andy that. He nearly told that old man out there everything we know about this," Shandra said, motioning to the tent flap.

"Shit!" Ryan stormed out of the tent and found Andy still talking to the old man.

"Andy."

The young man said good-bye to the old man and walked over. "Yeah?"

"We need to have a talk." By the time Ryan finished explaining how Andy needed to keep Millie safe and not tell anyone anything they knew about Lucille's death or what Millie knew, the others walked out of the tent.

"I'd like to get my things from my mother's tent and stay in this one. Is that all right?" Millie asked Logan.

"We are done looking for evidence. I don't see a problem with that." Logan started rolling up the crime scene tape.

"Shouldn't she stay near her family?" Andy asked.

"It would be better." Ryan studied the girl. He had

a feeling she hadn't told them everything.

"I don't like leaving Grandmother's tent untended. The materials in there are worth money. They are materials I can use to continue her work." Millie protested.

"I'll walk you back to your family, then I will stay in the tent at night. You can work on setting it up for the powwow during the day with me keeping watch." Andy put an arm around Millie's shoulders.

"That sounds like the best plan," Ryan said, grasping Shandra's hand. "Logan, see you tomorrow." He led his wife away from the three.

"Why did you leave so abruptly? We don't know if Millie will agree to that plan." Shandra walked beside him but her steps were sluggish.

"Because you need to rest, and I need to circle back and have a word with Andy."

Chapter Eight

The teepee had a gas lantern hanging from one of the poles. Mia was sound asleep in her bed. Aunt Jo stood from the folding chair she sat on, sewing beads on a band of buckskin.

Shandra wanted to shed her clothes, put on her pajamas, and drop onto the bed. Today had been mentally exhausting.

"How are things with Millie?" Aunt Jo asked.

"You know Andy is in love with her, don't you?" Shandra asked.

The woman smiled. "Yes, he has picked a good woman. She wants to carry on the ways of our people. And she has a kind heart."

Shandra smiled. "That's what I thought, too."

"And how are things with you?" Her aunt studied her.

"Good. I'm a bit confused about what I'm to do with the fur I found in my hand after my encounter with my wyakin." She started to put her hand in her pocket.

"No. Don't show me. I will give you a leather pouch tomorrow. You put the gift in the pouch and carry it with you. It will keep your guardian spirit close." Aunt Jo headed for the door. She glanced over her shoulder and smiled. "I knew you would be blessed with a wyakin."

She disappeared out the flap of the teepee.

Shandra knelt beside Mia, brushed a lock of hair from the child's cheek and leaned down to kiss the soft blush. She stood, put out the lantern, and disrobed, pulling on her pajamas and slipping into the sleeping bag.

"Grandmother will you come to me tonight in a dream to help solve Lucille's death?" she whispered and closed her eyes. Ella had never let her down when it came to helping Ryan solve a murder. She would come.

~*~

He'd told a small white lie, but it was for Shandra's own good. Ryan stood in the shadow of Lucille's tent. He'd arrived as Andy walked Millie back to her family. Ryan didn't know if someone would try to get in the tent when no one was around, however, he planned to be here if they did. From the things Millie didn't say, he had a feeling there was still something of value in the tent that whoever took the design would want. He hoped the woman would confide in Andy.

Waiting, he watched middle-aged and older people go in and out of the vendor tents in the area. Most seemed to be heading in for the night but a few men came back out, walking toward the area where the kids played stick games during the day. Martin told him that at night some of the men would play stick games and gamble. Shandra's uncle had said back in the days when bands and tribes would gather, they gambled on horse and foot races and games of sticks. Only then they gambled for furs, horses, and in some instances, captives, people they'd captured during raids.

It seemed all cultures had a penchant for gambling. He didn't understand it, but many of his fellow police officers over the years had spent a lot of the money they made on card games, sports games, and the lottery. Few had anything to show for it.

A movement to his left caught his attention. This person wasn't walking as if going somewhere, they lurked along the edges of tents, walking slowly, stopping at every tent. Just like the person Shandra had seen the night before.

Ryan didn't move, he hoped he was hidden in the shadow enough the individual wouldn't see him. He waited for the shadowed figure to approach Lucille's tent. One tent before it, the person slipped into a different tent. Giggling interrupted the silence around him. It appeared someone had planned a clandestine meeting. He wondered if this was the same skulker they'd seen leaving the area last night. There was one way to find out.

He walked over to the tent, rapped on the canvas, and called out, "Hello, could I speak to the person who just entered this tent."

"What do you want?" a male head appeared through the flap.

"Did you leave this tent about ten o'clock last night?" Ryan asked.

"What's it to you?" In the darkness it was hard to

tell the man's age, but his attitude and barely mature voice gave Ryan the feeling he was in his twenties or younger.

"If you were, I'll discount you as a murderer. If you weren't leaving this tent, then I'll need to take you to talk to Officer Rider." Ryan held up a hand as if to grasp the young man by the arm.

"He left here at ten. He had to get out before my mother came back," a teenage girl's voice said, before her head appeared underneath the young man's.

"Did either of you see or hear anything last night?" Ryan asked.

"Is this because of Lucille?" the girl asked.

"Yes. Did you see anything?"

"Millie was leaving there when I came to visit," the young man said.

"What time was that?" The coroner hadn't given them a time of death yet.

"I don't know, maybe eight-thirty or nine."

"I think closer to eight-thirty," the girl said.

"And you didn't see anyone else come or go?" Ryan didn't like that the granddaughter may have been the last to see her alive. He wondered if Logan knew about Millie visiting last night?

"Nothing else," they chorused.

"Ok. Thank you." He turned to leave.

"You won't tell anyone about…" The girl pointed up at the boy.

"No."

"Thank you."

Ryan walked back over to the side of Lucille's tent, then ducked inside. It looked as it had when he, Logan, and Millie had been in earlier.

The tent rustled and a sleeping bag shoved through the opening. Andy followed. Shock widened his eyes before curse words mumbled between his lips. When he'd gathered himself, he asked, "What are you doing in here?"

"I didn't want the tent left unattended until you returned." He unfolded a chair and sat. "Tell me about Lucille."

"I'm tired and I'm sure my mom knows more about her than I do." Andy moved some totes and laid out his sleeping bag.

"Did Millie tell Logan she was here last night?" Ryan decided to wake the young man up.

"What? No. I mean, I don't know. I wasn't with them all the time. How do you know that?"

Ryan tipped his head sideways. "The neighbors. They said she left here about eight-thirty."

"You and Shandra saw someone lurking around ten." He stared at Ryan as if daring him to correct that statement.

"We did. I also discovered it was possibly someone leaving from visiting the neighbors."

"How do you know these 'neighbors' are reliable?"

"I don't. Do you know who has the tent on that side?" He pointed toward the tent with the young couple.

"No. But I'll find out first thing tomorrow. Millie wouldn't hurt her grandmother."

"What about her brother? Would he?" Ryan had a gut feeling they hadn't killed their grandmother, but his gut also told him the granddaughter wasn't telling everything.

"Scott? No. But his wife isn't someone you'd want

64

to cross." Andy lay down on the sleeping bag. "You going to sleep with your wife tonight or me? Ays!"

"Smart ass. My wife. Make sure you don't sleep through someone tiptoeing around you." Ryan stood and exited the tent. He stopped, scanning the area and listening. Everyone had pretty much settled down for the night. There was a shout. He wandered that direction and found ten men still gambling.

He detoured and entered the teepee where his wife and daughter slept. This was a sight he'd almost given up hope of seeing. A daughter snug in her sleeping bag and his wife, waiting for him in their sleeping bag. He undressed and slid in with Shandra.

She woke up and wrapped an arm around his neck. "What took you so long?"

"I was waiting for Andy to return to the crime scene tent."

"Oh. You think someone missed what they were looking for?"

"I don't know. You had an exhausting day. We'll talk about it in the morning." Ryan kissed her and they snuggled together falling to sleep.

~*~

Shandra woke with a start.

"Get up sleepyhead!" Mia said, bouncing on her knees on the pad next to Shandra.

She glanced over and found Ryan gone. She remembered him coming to bed. "Where's Ryan?"

"He's eating breakfast. Aunt Jo told me to come wake you up. There is work to be done." Mia bounced then stopped. "Jayden wanted to help me wake you up but Aunt Jo said he couldn't come in because he was becoming a man." She shook her head. "He's still a

65

boy."

Shandra agreed. "There are some things that were good for the Nez Perce when they lived in villages and had to hunt, fish, and gather their food. Children like you and Jayden would be doing adult jobs because everyone had to help to survive. While we are here, Jayden will be treated differently, but when we get home, he will be the same goofy brother you love."

"Bleah! I don't love him. He's annoying."

Shandra laughed as Ryan walked into the teepee. "There's plenty of food still out there if you hurry."

"Aunt Jo made pancakes!" Mia shouted and ran out of the teepee.

Shandra laughed. "She is having a good time here."

"So is Jayden. I just hope all this 'he's a man' stuff doesn't go to his head." Ryan set the duffel bag with Shandra's clothes on the bed beside her.

"Me too. He had to be a man too early in his life, now he needs to be a boy." She pulled out a shirt and bra, exchanging those for her pajama top.

"We never had a chance to talk about your experience yesterday." Ryan peered down at her with concern on his face.

"It was fascinating. I wish I could tell you all about it, but—"

"I know. Martin and Jo told me not to bug you about it." He held her hands, helping her to stand.

She changed out of the pajama bottoms and into her jeans, which still held the fur from her guardian spirit. "Do you have any idea what we are doing today?"

"Not a clue. Though it does seem like another load of wood came in. It also needs split."

Shandra laughed at her husband's dejected expression. "Maybe Logan will show up and need your help."

They stepped out of the teepee. She noticed immediately that there were more people all over the grounds. The vendor tents were opening up and the bustle of people said they were going to do more than play Bingo today.

Aunt Jo walked up to her, handing her a small leather pouch. "Tonight will be the warm up and rejoining. We'll also have your naming ceremony. Be sure to wear this."

"You'll have to explain it all to me." Shandra followed her aunt over to the large griddle on a camp stove.

"We'll explain it to you as the day goes on. First you must eat." Jo piled three pancakes on a plate for her and four on a plate for Ryan.

They moved on to the table with plates of bacon and eggs, huckleberry syrup, and butter.

"It's probably a good thing they have me helping set up the chairs at the arbor. It will work off all the food your aunt is feeding us," Ryan said.

"Today is the last day we all eat together. When the dancing starts the women are busy," Uncle Lloyd said, as they sat at a table.

"That makes sense. I imagine they will be busy getting their children and themselves ready for the dances." Shandra smeared the huckleberry syrup around on her pancakes.

"Dancing is a time to give thanks to the Creator and heal." Lloyd picked up his cup of coffee and sipped.

Shandra wondered at the use of healing in terms of the dancing. That's what Mia had said Aunt Jo told her about the Jingle Dance.

Before she could open her mouth to ask a question, Millie ran over to them.

"Andy needs help."

Ryan jumped up, and Shandra followed him toward the vendor tents. When they arrived at Lucille's tent, Andy stumbled out of it. Blood trickled down his face.

Before he fell forward, Ryan caught him, gently lying her cousin onto his back. "Call for EMTs," Ryan said.

Shandra pulled out her phone and dialed 9-1-1.

"What happened?" Ryan asked, peering up at Millie who stood back, tears streaming down her face.

"I don't know. I came to set up to sell today and found him on his sleeping bag with blood…" Her gaze flashed to Andy and back to Ryan.

"Damn! I was right. What else was in that tent that you knew about and so did the person who killed your grandmother?" Ryan stood, facing the sobbing girl.

Shandra put a hand on his arm. "Now may not be the time to do this."

A crowd had gathered.

Two people parted the crowd. They had on shirts showing they were EMTs.

"What happened?" the older of the two men asked.

"I found him unconscious in there." Millie pointed to the tent.

They checked his vital signs, cleaned the wound, and said they were taking him to the clinic.

Shandra looked up as Aunt Jo pushed through the

crowd. "What happened to my boy?"

"He'll be fine." Shandra put an arm around her aunt, keeping her from getting in the EMTs way.

"They're taking him to the clinic," Millie said, glancing over her shoulder at the tent and then down at Andy.

"You two go with him. Ryan and I will watch the tent," Shandra said, receiving a nod from her husband.

The EMTs helped a now conscious Andy onto their gurney.

"I should..." Millie glanced at the tent, then the gurney moving through the crowd.

"You aren't going to lose that much business by staying with Andy for the morning," Shandra said. "Go with him. I'll be right here when you get back and I'll help you open up."

"Thank you." The girl hugged her quickly and ran after the gurney and Aunt Jo.

Ryan stepped around her. "It's all over. Go on about your day!" He waved his hands and the crowd slowly dispersed.

"You should call Logan," Shandra suggested.

"That's my plan. After we take a quick look inside." Ryan held the flap back for her to enter.

The contents had been strewn about. From the smear of blood on the outside of Andy's sleeping bag, he'd either struggled with the intruder or had been knocked out before he saw them and fell onto his makeshift bed.

"They were definitely looking for something." Ryan pulled out his phone and took photos from various angles. "I hope those weren't expensive. It's going to be hard to gather all the beads out of the dirt."

"Do you think they will look for fingerprints?" Shandra scanned the upturned drawers pulled out of plastic storage units.

"I'm pretty sure whoever did this had on gloves, but I'll ask Logan. Don't touch anything until I talk with him." Ryan scrolled on his phone and then started talking. "Logan, Ryan. Someone ransacked the Lightning tent and hit Andy over the head." He listened as Shandra stood from her crouched position and studied the mess.

"I took photos. There are beads everywhere. Do you want to send someone to check for prints?" He listened and nodded his head. "Ok. Shandra told Millie she'd get things cleaned up while she was with Andy at the clinic. Are you giving her a go-ahead to do that?" He listened some more. "We won't touch anything that is near the scene of the attack or that might have been a weapon." Ryan shoved his phone in his holster.

"Did he say we could pick up the beads?" Shandra asked, ready to get started.

"I'll get some tape and make a circle around Andy's bedding. Logan doesn't want anything there disturbed. He said beads can be picked up but try not to touch anything that might have been used as a weapon."

"We can work on that mess over there by the door until Logan is finished." Shandra had spotted a pile of the smallest beads on the ground near the door as she'd listened to Ryan's conversation.

"When you get the crime tape bring Mia and Jayden back with you." Shandra picked up a plastic container with drawers. She wouldn't know what went where, but they could get them off the ground.

"Looking at the mess, I hope whoever did this

found what they were looking for, or you three won't be safe in here." Ryan put a hand on the tent flap. "Be careful while I get the kids."

Shandra nodded and continued setting bead containers up where they had been opened or overturned near piles of beads. What could the person want that would be hidden with beads? What did Lucille have that was worth killing for? Surely not a contract with a reputable gallery. A gallery would know her work and want that, not someone else's. And a design… that didn't make sense even though Millie seemed to think that was behind her grandmother's death.

The tent wiggled before the twins and Fawn burst through the door.

"Whoa! Be careful. See all the beads on the ground? We need to pick them all up. Start at the pile closest to you and put them in a container near that pile." She smiled as the three dropped to their knees without a complaint and started picking up beads.

Mia 'ooed and awed' over the colors and showed them to Fawn as she put them in the containers.

"Why are Millie's beads on the ground?" Fawn asked.

"Someone came in and made the mess." Shandra avoided saying her father was in here when it happened. She picked up several piles then started putting the filled containers into an empty tote. She wanted to pick up the finished products strewn about, but knew those pieces could have evidence on them.

Male voices approached. She recognized Ryan's voice. Within seconds, both Logan and Ryan entered the tent.

"Hey! I said you could pick up beads too small to have a fingerprint on them," Logan said, a frown on his usually jolly face.

"We've only been picking up containers that we filled and putting them in an empty tote. The rest we haven't touched." Shandra straightened and peered at Logan. "If we wait to pick up the beads after a whole crew of forensic people come in here, Millie won't have anything left to work with."

"I took photos before they started cleaning up," Ryan said, holding up his phone. "You can see, Shandra has touched very little." The two looked at the photos making comments.

"Have you found anything interesting?" Logan asked Shandra.

She waved her hands. "Thank you for your help, kids. Why don't you three go play now?"

When the kids had left, she said, "Nothing. I don't understand what a beadwork artist would have that someone would kill for." Shandra stood. "Is there anything else Lucille was into that could be the cause of her death?"

"So far, I haven't learned anything." Logan studied the mess. "I hope whoever did this found what they wanted. I don't want anyone else hurt."

Chapter Nine

Half of the beads were picked up when Millie
returned around noon. Andy was with her, his head
bandaged. Fawn ran up to him, hugging him around the
waist.

"What happened, Daddy?" she asked as Jayden and
Mia moved closer to Shandra.

"I fell and hurt my head. I'm better now." Andy
made his way across the tent to a folding chair Logan
had used while taking notes.

"I'm going to take the kids to get some lunch and
then I'll come back," Shandra said. "Will you three be
okay?"

Millie nodded. "Thank you all for picking up the
beads."

"It was fun!" Mia said.

Jayden nodded, his gaze on Andy. "Are you
okay?"

Andy gave him a lopsided grin. "Yeah." He ran a

hand down Fawn's hair as she sat on his lap.

"Did Logan already ask you questions?" Shandra asked, moving the twins toward the tent opening.

"Yeah. I told him what little I know." He glanced up at Millie. "Some protector I am."

"Shh… I'd rather lose whatever it was the person took than you." She put a hand on his shoulder.

Her cousin's face beamed with happiness. This seemed to be bringing the two closer, but it was a tough way to do it. "I'll be back in thirty minutes Do you want me to take Fawn with us?" Shandra asked.

"Do you want to go get some lunch?" Millie asked the child.

She nodded.

"I'll see if your mom can watch her after she eats," Shandra said, herding the kids out of the tent.

"Can I come back with you?" Mia asked.

"Me, too!" Fawn exclaimed.

"We'll see. It will depend on if Aunt Jo needs your help." Shandra could see Mia was interested in beading. It would be good for her to sit with Millie and learn about it.

"After I eat, I'm going to find Uncle Martin and see what he needs help with," Jayden said with more importance than usual.

"That sounds like a good idea," Shandra's mind kept spinning the fact Andy had been hurt and Ella hadn't come to her in any dreams to help with any clues. She thought being here, on the reservation, close to family, Ella would have been in and out of her thoughts and dreams more.

"There you four are. We have sandwiches for lunch." Aunt Jo motioned to a tray with a towel over it.

They walked over and plucked halves of sandwiches from the tray and placed them on napkins.

"Would you like iced tea, lemonade, or water?" Aunt Jo asked.

They all picked water.

"How bad was Andy hurt?" Shandra asked when the twins and Fawn wandered off to sit with some of the other children.

"They put a couple stitches on the gash. I don't know if I'm happy he didn't see anyone, or not. If he had, this whole thing could be cleared up. But at the same time had he seen who hit him, he could end up like poor Lucille." Aunt Jo sat down next to Shandra with a glass of iced tea.

She patted her aunt's arm. "I know. I kept thinking that as I picked up the beads. Do you have any idea what Lucille could have had that someone wanted bad enough to kill her?"

"I've been thinking about it and I can't think of anything. She was a good person. She helped others. I never heard her raise her voice to anyone. Not even Morton or Marian. Though you could see by the color on Lucille's cheeks and the sparks in her eyes, she wished to say something."

That caught Shandra's attention. "What angered Lucille about Scott's wife?"

"Marian wanted Lucille to invest in her horse training and not the cultural center."

"Marian is selfish where Lucille was selfless." Shandra said.

"Yes. Lucille was true to her people. Marian has only cared about her culture to use it to get more horses to train. But her ways are not that of our people." Aunt

Jo stared off toward the arbor. "She doesn't participate in anything around here unless it will show off her horses."

"Where did she and Scott meet?" Shandra wondered if Marian was from the reservation.

"At the Omak Stampede three years ago. They were both competing. Marian is from somewhere around Seattle. She claims to have Indian blood, but she hasn't acted like it." Aunt Jo usually talked about everyone in a good light.

"Is there proof that Lucille wanted to help the community center? Who would Logan need to talk to about a will?"

Aunt Jo studied Shandra. "Very few people of Lucille's age think to have a will. At her death, the land, her money, and the beadwork would go to her daughter."

Shandra thought back to what she'd heard about the family. "The one who doesn't live here?"

"Yes."

"If there isn't a will, Scott and Millie would have nothing, unless the daughter is generous?" She glanced at her aunt to see her reaction.

"I have no idea what Geri will do. She graduated from school and left here as fast as the bus would take her. I don't even know where she ended up or what she does." Jo stared over toward the arbor. "Geri was a really good dancer."

"Does she come to the powwow?" Shandra thought that would make it easier to talk to her and get some answers.

"No. She hasn't come back for anything that I know of."

Shandra knew where she could find out some of her answers. Back at the vendor tent with Millie and Andy. "I promised Millie I'd come back and help her set things up. See you tonight."

Aunt Jo shook her head. "You can only help her until four or five at the latest. You'll need to get changed and ready for the warm-up, rejoining, and naming ceremony."

"I thought the dancing wasn't until tomorrow." Shandra wasn't ready to go public with the little bit she'd learned of the Jingle Dance or her experience yesterday.

"It all starts tonight. The warm-up would be good for you and Mia to get used to the music and the pace of the dances. You don't want to look like first timers when you compete."

"I don't plan on going in any competitions. Just dressing up for the grand entries." Shandra was excited to dance in full regalia and hear the beat of the drums, but she wasn't competing. She was nowhere near the caliber of the other dancers.

"I entered you in the adult competition and Mia in the juniors on Saturday at one. That is usually when the new dancers compete. You'll be fine. I can help you get dressed tonight." Aunt Jo shooed her away.

Shandra headed to Lucille's tent wondering if Logan had started the ball rolling to contact Geri.

~*~

Ryan was impressed with how much information Logan could get out of people with his affable smile and easy-going manner. They were visiting with Millie's mom's side of the family.

"Did Lucille confide in any of you about what her

plans were for her land when she traveled to the Creator?" Logan asked.

Millie's grandmother from her mom's side cleared her throat. "The last time Lucille came by to visit, she said she'd had a long discussion with herself and knew what she wanted to do. She said Morton Yellowtail wouldn't be happy, but she didn't care."

"What would her determining what to do with her estate have to do with Morton?" Logan asked.

Ryan was thinking the same thing. He wasn't family that he'd heard.

Another woman leaned forward in her fold-up camp chair. "Ever since Lucille talked about leaving something to the Cultural Center, Morton has been trying to talk her into saying it was to be used however the board saw fit." She shook her head. "Lucille didn't believe teaching our youth computers would help them keep traditions."

"Lucille believed if we lose our traditions, we lose ourselves," Millie's grandmother said.

Logan nodded. "Have any of you heard where Geri is?"

Ryan stared at Logan. Where had he pulled that name from? He hadn't heard it before.

"Millie or Scott might know. No one in the family talked much about her," another woman said.

"Ok. Thanks." Logan placed his hat on his head and walked away.

Ryan followed. "Who is Geri?"

"Lucille's only living child. Her daughter who left here as soon as she graduated high school." Logan strode back through the family camps toward the vendor area. "If Lucille didn't leave a will, which a lot of the older people don't, everything will go to Geri."

"From what the women back there said, it sounds like Lucille must have something written up." Ryan wondered if that was what the intruder was looking for last night.

"I need to find out from Millie or Scott if they know anything about it." Logan shook his head. "As much as I think Morton is a big-mouthed pain in the rear, I can't see him killing Lucille by strangulation. He would have gotten queasy before he finished the job." The big tribal policeman stopped and peered at Ryan. "But I could see him sneaking in last night looking for the papers, and when Andy started moving, hitting him from behind."

"That would mean Morton knows about the paper Lucille had written up." Ryan wondered if she'd confided in anyone else. "Did Lucille have a best friend?"

"After we talk to Millie and Scott that's where I planned to go next." Logan grinned and resumed walking.

The tent where the body had been found and Andy had been assaulted, had the front opened up with a canopy set up. Tables with beadwork under glass cases lined the two sides of the area. Shandra, Millie, and Andy sat in chairs back by the tent.

Logan took his time viewing the beadwork.

Ryan glanced in a couple of cases as he made his way to his wife. "You guys did a lot of work to get this all set up."

"Andy follows directions better when he's been hit on the head," Shandra joked.

"Hey!" Andy protested, and Logan laughed.

"He always does a good job when he works with me," Millie said, her cheeks flushing.

"I'm sure he does. Who wouldn't want to help a pretty girl?" Logan said. He turned his attention to the young woman. "Do you know if your grandmother had a will or some other legal document drawn up about how her land, money, and business would be dealt with at her death?"

Millie drew in a deep breath. "She told me the beadwork business would go to me and the land was to be sold with that money being split between Scott, Aunt Geri, and the Cultural Center." She glanced at each of them, her gaze resting on Andy. "But I don't know if she made it legal or if it was ever written down."

"Who else knew of her wishes?" Logan asked.

Millie shrugged. "I told Scott and I assume he told Marian. As for Geri, I don't know. There is an address for her in Grandmother's things but I don't know how old it is."

"What about people at the Cultural Center?" Ryan asked. While he concurred with Logan that Morton Yellowtail most likely didn't kill the woman, he would be interested in the outcome of her estate.

Millie shook her head. "That I don't know. I'd think your mom," she leveled her gaze on Andy, "would know that."

"She hasn't said anything, but Mom is good at keeping things to herself." Andy reached out, grasping Millie's hand.

"Where would I find this last address for your aunt?" Logan asked.

"At the house. Scott should be able to get it for you."

"What about Marian? Does she know how to contact your aunt?" Ryan asked.

"I don't know. Probably if Scott told her." Millie studied Logan. "Do you think Aunt Geri killed Grandmother?"

"No. But I'd like to know if she had any idea what your grandmother was doing with her belongings." Logan headed out of the small vendor booth.

"Mind if I ride along?" Ryan asked.

"Mia and I will be in the warm-up dance tonight at seven. And my naming ceremony is tonight," Shandra said.

Ryan focused on the tribal policeman. "Will we be back by then?"

"We should be." Logan grinned. "Unless you'd rather stay away longer? Ays?"

"I'll be back in time. See you then or earlier." Ryan leaned down, kissed his wife on the cheek, and hurried after Logan, striding through the tents on a mission.

Chapter Ten

Logan crossed the powwow grounds quickly.

Ryan stayed up with him stride for stride. "Where are we going? I thought you wanted to get the aunt's address from Scott?"

"We're going to talk to someone who knew Lucille well. My ella." Logan slowed down as they entered another family camp. Every person they passed greeted the tribal policeman. Some with sarcasm and jokes. He nodded or replied back, slowing even more before he stopped in front of a woman who had to be in her nineties if not one hundred.

"Ella, this is Shandra Higheagle's husband," Logan introduced him.

"Mrs. Rider, it's a pleasure to see you again," Ryan said, holding out a hand. He'd met this woman before his marriage when Shandra visited her.

Mrs. Rider raised the gnarled hand on her cane and waved his hand away. "The grandson of my best friend would never shake hands. He would embrace me."

Ryan glanced at Logan who nodded. He leaned down, giving the woman a soft hug. She was all bones and smelled of sage.

When he straightened, a welcoming smile curved her lips and her eyes sparkled.

"Now I believe you are the grandson of my best friend. Why has my grandson brought you to me?"

"Ella, we need to know anything you can tell us about Lucille Lightning," Logan said, drawing the woman's gaze.

"She was a good woman. Her life was taken too soon. Just like Minnie." The woman closed her eyes and her lips moved.

Ryan started to open his mouth. Logan bumped him with a fist, shaking his head when Ryan glanced at him.

"Lucille was a kind woman who gave back to The People. She wished the youth to continue to learn the old ways. She told me she went to Liz Piney to help her draw up her wishes. Though she didn't plan on leaving this earth this soon."

"That's Shandra's cousin," Ryan said, remembering how she'd helped when Coop had been a murder suspect.

"She is. And a fine young woman." The old woman stared pointedly at her grandson.

"Thank you for this information, Ella." Logan leaned down and kissed his grandmother's cheek. "Come on. We have a stop to make before we go to the Lightning Ranch and get you back here in time for your wife's naming ceremony."

"I heard about that. It's about time Shandra

Paty Jager

received her Nez Perce name." Mrs. Rider motioned for the two to get going.

Logan marched out behind his family's camp and there stood a tribal police vehicle. "Get in. I doubt Liz is at work. But she'll be here tonight. For the naming ceremony and the warm up."

"I'm surprised I haven't seen her at the family camp," Ryan said.

"She was probably working. Her hours are as busy as mine. That's why my grandmother hasn't seen me dating Liz." He winked.

Ryan laughed. "Are you going to be a relative one of these days?"

"If things keep progressing."

"That will make Shandra very happy." Ryan couldn't wait to tell Shandra her favorite policeman, next to him, would be marrying one of her favorite cousins.

~*~

Returning to the Lightning Beadworks booth, Shandra took care in checking out all the vendors around them. Ryan had told her about his and Velma's talk with Kitty Waters, Lucille's competitor. The path she took through the vendors hadn't passed anyone with beadwork.

"Hey, good to see you back. I need to run to the restroom but didn't want to leave Andy alone." Millie stood as Shandra entered the booth.

"Do you have prices on everything?" Shandra asked, studying the beading in the glass cases and the containers of beads and thread.

"Everything is marked on the cases. "These are twenty dollars, forty, fifty, and so on. The beads and thread are also marked either on the tubes or next to where the hanks hang. Don't let anyone get their own. That way you can see the price and they can't say it came from a cheaper one." She glanced at Andy and smiled. "He's been helping all morning and knows everything."

Shandra smiled at her cousin's embarrassment. "Take your time."

When Millie was out of earshot, Shandra asked, "Has Millie said anything about what she thinks happened to her grandmother or who would have been looking for something in the tent last night?"

Andy shrugged. "She thinks it probably has something to do with the paper her grandmother had drawn up. She told the family about it last weekend."

"Family? Scott, his wife, and Millie?"

"Yeah. I don't think she had time to contact her daughter, Geri. It sounds like Lucille only signed the paperwork last Friday."

Two people wandered into the booth, browsing along the glass boxes.

"These are beautiful. Did you make them?" the older of the two women asked.

"No. They were made by Lucille Lightning." Shandra saw the pile of brochures and business cards. She wondered if that was Lucille's idea or Millie's. She picked up a brochure and handed it to the lady.

"This work is beautiful." The woman took the brochure, scanned the contents, and continued to browse the boxes.

Millie returned.

"This is the artist's granddaughter who also does beading." Shandra motioned for Millie to speak with the woman.

Being an artist herself, she understood that while you may not like to talk up your art, it was crucial if you wished to be paid and continue doing what you loved.

She listened to Millie describe the type of beadwork and the story that was told in the beading. The woman ended up spending over two hundred dollars and saying she'd be in touch.

Millie sat down holding her phone that she'd used for the transaction. "That was our biggest sale today. Hopefully, there will be more and Grandmother's art will make many people happy."

Shandra patted the young woman's knee. "She would want her art to be appreciated."

"I know. She talked about this powwow all year. She makes special pieces for each powwow. This one she has several medallions and some earrings. Being on the Powwow committee, she knows the colors that will be used on promotional material and uses those in her pieces."

"That's smart. Did she come up with that on her own or did you help her?"

"I thought of it. She was also eager to get a website, use an online store to sell things, and the brochures and business cards were my idea. She's been making twice as much as she was before we went online. She was happy to do the beading and teach me and let me deal with the rest." Millie sighed. "I don't have the instinct she did for colors and patterns. I don't know if I'll be able to keep the business going trying to do both the beading and the marketing."

It was easy to see that Millie would not have killed

her grandmother. She had the most to lose from the loss. "I'm sure you'll figure out something." Shandra glanced at Andy. "You know, he has a brother who works with computers and he has a pretty good knowledge of them, too. Maybe Andy could take on some of the computer stuff and you can concentrate on learning more about beading?"

Millie locked gazes with Andy. "Would you help me?"

"Yeah."

Some more people wandered into the booth. Shandra stayed put as Millie walked over and started visiting with them.

"If you need help with anything related to art and galleries, let me know," she said quietly to Andy.

He grinned. "Thanks for giving me more of a reason to hang around with her."

"You're welcome. I have a question for you. What happens at a naming ceremony?"

Chapter Eleven

Ryan was impressed with the Lightning Ranch. The main house, smaller house to the side, barn, and corrals were all freshly painted and showing hardly any wear and tear. "Lucille must have made good money with her beadwork."

Logan parked the vehicle. "Scott has done all the work to make this place shine. Lucille gave him money but it is all his sweat."

They stepped out of the tribal vehicle as two dogs raced out of the barn area, barking.

"Hey boys, good guys here," Logan said in his friendly voice.

Ryan was getting ready to hop back in the vehicle when the two slid to a stop and looked up at Logan as if he were their master.

"Where's Scott?" Logan asked the dogs.

They swished their feathered tails back and forth across the gravel, their tongues hanging out.

A movement in the direction the dogs had come, caught Ryan's attention. He glanced over and Scott came around the side of the barn with a woman dressed like a western Barbie. The pant legs of her tight jeans were tucked into tall expensive boots. He knew they were expensive because they looked like a pair his boot-loving wife had in their closet. Her western-cut long-sleeved shirt was tailored to show off her curves. Her long blonde hair fell in waves around her shoulders under a bright white straw cowboy hat.

Now he knew why the ranch was in pristine shape, he had a feeling Scott's wife was the one who kept after him.

"Scott, Marian, I have some questions for you concerning Lucille," Logan said, motioning to the house.

"Sure, anything we can do to help." Scott changed direction, heading to the front of the house. "I still can't believe someone… you know."

Marian didn't say anything, she just fell into step behind Scott.

Once they were all seated in the kitchen where Scott poured everyone a cup of coffee, Logan started, "I'd like your Aunt Geri's address, please."

"Oh, sure. I hadn't thought about trying to contact her. She's never around so I don't think about her." Scott set the last cup of coffee in front of his wife. "I think her address is in Grandma's address book. I'll go get it."

As soon as he left the room, Logan studied Marian. "Have you any idea why someone would want to kill Lucille?"

She didn't flinch or bat an eye. "She was a sweet

woman. No. I can't think of any reason."

"But you and she didn't get along," Ryan said.

She focused on him. "Excuse me? Who are you?"

"He's a consulting detective," Logan said as Scott returned to the kitchen.

"I think this is the last address Grandmother had for Geri." He slid the open book across the table to Logan.

The tribal policeman wrote down the address and closed the book before sliding it back across the table. "Thank you. Did either of you know about a will your grandmother had Liz Piney draw up?"

"Yeah. She told us about it over the weekend. I thought it was fair. Didn't expect the paper to be necessary this soon." Scott shoved a hand over his face and through his short dark hair.

Marian put a hand on his back. "Lucille was healthy as a horse. No one expected something like this to happen."

"What I understand, you'll have to sell this place and split the money three ways, are you going to be okay with that?" Logan asked.

Scott shook his head. "I'm hoping Aunt Geri will let us stay, I can possibly get the third that would go to the center together and then pay Geri over time. I really don't want to lose the family ranch."

"Scott has put a lot of work into this place. It would be a shame for us to lose it over a piece of paper." Marian picked up her coffee, hiding her lower face behind the cup.

"A will is binding. You'll have to sell," Ryan said.

"We'll see," Marian said, standing. "I need to get back to the horses." She spun around and walked out of the house.

"What did she mean by 'we'll see?'" Ryan asked Scott.

"She keeps saying things could work out. That's what I love about her. She is an eternal optimist."

Ryan stared at the man. That wasn't the feeling the woman gave him. She was a manipulator. Had she been the one to sneak into the tent, bash Andy in the head, and perhaps take off with the will, thinking with that copy gone there wouldn't be another one?

"Thank you for your time," Logan said, standing and reaching a hand across the table to the grandson.

"I hope you find out who did this. I can't think of anyone who would hate Grandmother enough to…" Scott ran a hand over his face. "Sorry. She has always been here for us to lean on. I'm thankful for Marian. She's tough. It's what I need. Let me know if you contact Aunt Geri and if she needs me to do anything."

"I will." Logan put his hat on his head and walked to the back door. "You and Millie were the best thing that ever happened to Lucille after losing her two sons."

Scott nodded.

Ryan followed Logan to the vehicle. Once they were seated inside, he spoke. "Did you get the same vibe from Marian?"

"That she did something to the will?" Logan started the SUV.

"Yeah."

"We'll go find Liz and see what she has to say." Logan shot him a lopsided smile. "I think I'll visit with her by myself."

Ryan grinned. "I don't see a problem with that. I need to find my wife and settle her nerves."

~*~

Mia was practicing her dancing in the teepee wearing the beautiful dress Aunt Jo had made for her.

"You look adorable in that," Shandra told her as she pressed a hand to her wringing stomach. The dancing wasn't the part that bothered her. It was standing in front of her family and strangers and telling of her encounter with her guardian spirit. How would anyone believe her? She'd attached the leather pouch with the fur to the beaded belt of her dress.

Ryan entered the teepee and stopped inside the entrance. "You two will be the most beautiful dancers tonight." He crossed the space between them to lay a hand on Mia's head and then kiss Shandra's cheek.

"You're biased," she said.

"What does that mean?" Mia asked, stopping her dancing feet and watching them.

"It means, because Ryan loves us, he believes we are more beautiful than anyone else." Shandra rubbed a hand up and down his arm. "But I am grateful for your presence. I don't remember when I've been this nervous about anything."

"You'll be fine. Did your aunt explain the whole ceremony to you?" Ryan led her over to the two folding chairs.

She hiked up the dress, revealing leggings underneath, and sat.

Ryan sat in the chair beside her, clasping one of her hands in his.

"She said, everyone in the family brought gifts that will be given to everyone who attends the ceremony-family and strangers alike. I am to sing of my encounter with my wyakin." She clenched his hand. "That is what

I don't know how to do. I don't know the language. What if what I say sounds crazy?"

"Hey, I'm sure everyone here, besides your immediate family, has witnessed a name ceremony and won't find what you say 'crazy.'" Ryan kissed her cheek. "You'll be fine. How about this. I think it will cheer you up. I think your cousin Liz and Logan are dating."

Shandra's heart burst with happiness for two people she had connected with during Coop's ordeal. "That's wonderful!"

"But he's keeping it quiet for a while yet. I think because while they are dating, he's not sure how their two busy lives will mesh." Ryan was about to lean in for a kiss when someone called out, "Knock. Knock."

Shandra spun to the door and watched as Coop, several years older and more mature, walked in, followed by Sandy, his wife.

"Coop! I didn't think you were coming until tomorrow." Shandra rushed across the room giving both he and Sandy a hug.

"You don't think I'd miss my favorite cousin's naming ceremony." Coop grinned from ear to ear.

He was a welcome sight. Back when she'd first met him, they'd formed a bond that was more like brother and sister than cousins. "I'm so nervous. I can't sing."

"Then tell it like a poem." Coop studied her. "Close your eyes when you are standing there, see the meeting, and describe the moment."

"I told you, you were overthinking this," Ryan said from behind her.

"Thank you. You're the first one to make it sound

easy." Shandra laughed nervously. She really looked at them for the first time since their entrance. "Why aren't you dressed to dance?"

"We'll wait until the competitions that start tomorrow," Sandy said.

"Who is this beautiful princess?" Coop asked, pointing at Mia.

"Mia, come meet my cousins, Coop and Sandy." Shandra motioned for her daughter to come forward.

"Coop. That's where chickens stay," Mia said, studying the couple.

Coop burst out laughing. "It is. Coop is short for Cooper."

"If Shandra likes you, then I like you." Mia stuck out her hand and shook with both Sandy and Coop.

Aunt Jo stuck her head in the teepee. "Come on. The evening is beginning."

Chapter Twelve

While Shandra and Mia stood in line for the grand entry, Ryan looked for Logan. If Liz was dancing tonight, he figured the tribal policeman would be sticking around.

While he scanned the area for a uniform, someone came up behind him, pulling on his shirt tail. Ryan spun around and found Jayden dressed in regalia.

"I didn't know you were dancing tonight as well," he said, putting a hand on the boy's shoulder.

"Andy said because he can't yet with his stiches, he wanted me to go in for him. But I don't want to walk in alone." This was the first time this week Jayden was showing his true age.

"Let's go see if we can find your sister and Shandra." Ryan grasped the boy's hand and led him to where he'd left his wife and daughter.

"You looking for someone to walk with?" Logan asked.

Ryan faced the voice and found the tribal policeman in regalia. "Whoa. I didn't know you were dancing tonight as well."

"It's a healing thing. Doing this job, I need it." He motioned to Jayden to follow him. "Come on. Just do what I do."

"Did you get a chance to talk to Liz?" Ryan asked.

"Not yet. We can meet after the naming ceremony. You, me, Shandra, and Liz." He disappeared among other people dressed in regalia. Jayden was right behind him.

It looked like all he could do right now was sit and watch the event. Walking along the upper edge of the three feet high cement block wall that circled the arbor, he spotted Andy sitting by himself.

"Where is everyone?" Ryan asked.

"Dad is rounding up all the gifts for Shandra's naming ceremony. Mom, Millie, and Fawn are down there dancing, and Coop and Sandy went to find something to eat." Andy rubbed the bandage on his head. "If Mom hadn't heard the doctor say nothing physical for twenty-four hours, I'd be out there dancing, too."

"How long will this last?" Ryan was thinking about the information they'd get from Liz.

"If it starts on time, a couple hours. Then we'll have the naming ceremony. That will last as long as it takes for Shandra to sing, Mom to give her her name, and to hand out the gifts." Andy relaxed back into the camp chair he sat in. "You might as well relax and watch your family."

Ryan decided that would be better than wondering which direction they needed to go to figure out the homicide.

~*~

Shandra gave Liz a hug when they were standing in line waiting to enter the arbor. "I have no idea what I'm doing," she confessed.

"Just watch me. Tonight is just a test run. Since you are in a Jingle dress, you must dance the Jingle Dance. Aunt Jo is dancing traditional. Don't do what she does."

Shandra squeezed Mia's hand to get her attention. "Did you hear Liz? She says only dance like the girls who are wearing a Jingle dress."

"I will. Aunt Jo and Fawn told me that already. When do we get to go in?" Mia whined the last part.

"When they are ready for us." Shandra craned her neck trying to see where Ryan had sat.

"They are waiting for all the drummers to arrive," Liz said. "A good dancer uses the beat of the drum to move their feet. It is the heart beat of Mother Earth."

"Really?" Mia moved closer to Liz. "Have you seen Mother Earth?"

"No, but I've seen the great bounties she's given us. Fish, berries, vegetables, meat. She provides the means for all our food to grow. And gives us water and shade when it is hot."

"What about when it's cold?" Mia asked.

That's when Shanda spotted Ryan and Andy. She waved and he waved back, smiling.

"Hello ladies," Logan's voice spun Shandra around, but not before she saw her cousin's eyes light up.

The policeman stood behind them dressed in full regalia. Jayden stood beside him.

"Why do you have string all over you?" Mia asked.

"Because I'm a grass dancer. These strings represent grass." Logan touched her nose. "You are a very pretty Jingle dancer."

"What about me?" Jayden asked.

Shandra put a hand on his shoulder. "You are a handsome grass dancer." It appeared Aunt Jo had made Jayden a ribbon shirt and leggings with string on the side seams like fringe.

"But grass isn't all those colors," Mia said.

"It depends on the light, where you are, and how you look at it." Logan moved he and Jayden passed them. "Sorry, men enter first." His gaze met Liz's as he passed her.

"Did Logan and Ryan talk to you about Lucille's will?" Shandra wondered what that outcome had been.

"No. That must be what Logan meant when he asked me to meet with all of you after this."

The MC called for the head women and men to enter.

"I'll tell you what I know afterward," Liz said as the drums beat and the singer wailed.

Mia tugged on Shandra's sleeve. "Is that the music we dance to?"

"Yes." The group started moving into the arbor. Shandra kept track of Mia and they jingled their way into the arbor and danced around the circular area. She caught sight of Liz once, watched how light she was on her feet and then caught a glimpse of Logan. Jayden danced by her, a huge smile on his face. She glanced up at Ryan as she danced by. He smiled. Coop and Sandy waved.

The group was asked to leave the arbor and the MC

announced new members of the Confederated Tribes of the Colville. When that finished, Shandra heard her name called. Her stomach twisted and she forgot to breathe.

"Come on. You'll be fine," Aunt Jo had a hold of her arm, escorting her to the stage where the elder, being the MC for the event, stood. All her family followed. Ryan and the twins behind her and then her uncles, aunts, and cousins.

"We have been told you were taken from us when your father went to the Creator and now you have returned. Your family believes you deserve a Nez Perce name."

"Yes." She was surprised the word came out so clear. Her throat felt about as big around as a pencil.

"I was also told you have gone on a vision quest. Before you are named, you will sing of your wyakin." He handed her the microphone.

She'd never held one before. Her hands shook, clasping the microphone in front of her. If she looked around at the crowd still around the arbor, she'd faint. She found Ryan, Mia, and Jayden standing near the stage. Staring at them, she told of her encounter with her guardian spirit. "The silver wolf said to me, "*Keep your cubs close, help them grow, teach them how to survive.*"

As the words rang out through the arbor, she realized that the most important thing to her was to raise the two children that had come into her life, teach them her culture, and help guide other youth to learn their true selves.

Aunt Jo walked over, gave her a hug, and took the microphone. "Her family has decided on this name for our sister. Lost One Follows Heart. *Peléy 'áyat kiyé-twikse ku ti 'mine.*"

"Thank you, Aunt Jo." She faced the people watching. "And all my family!"

A roar went up.

Jo said the crowd was to come down and get their gifts.

The people entered the arbor, formed a large circle, and sidestepped around to greet Shandra, shaking her hand. She only knew a handful of the family members. Others were members of the community.

When the pile of gifts grew smaller, Aunt Jo said. "You can go now. I'm so happy you had a good vision quest. The words of your guardian spirit are wise."

"I know. I understand what they mean. See you tomorrow." She gave her aunt a one-armed hug.

Ryan appeared at her side. "I'm proud of you." He kissed her temple.

"Thanks. Are Liz and Logan waiting for me?"

"They went to change. They're coming to our teepee when they're done."

"Where are the twins?" she asked as they walked out of the arbor.

"Coop and Sandy took them. They didn't say what they were doing, but Jayden was excited." Ryan led her straight to their teepee. "I figured you'd want to get out of that before our company arrives."

"Yes. I can't sit when I'm wearing this." Shandra quickly drew the dress over her head and slipped into a tunic that reached nearly to her knees over the leggings.

"I don't understand what is taking them so long." Ryan had talked with Logan as he'd left the arbor. The tribal officer had made it sound like he and Liz would be waiting for Ryan and Shandra at the teepee. He walked to the tent flap and looked out.

"Maybe they're enjoying each other's company." Shandra walked up behind Ryan. "Do you know where they were changing their clothes?"

"No. I'm going to give Logan a call." He pulled out his phone and scrolled down his list of contacts.

The phone rang several times and Logan answered out of breath.

"What's going on?" Ryan asked.

"Someone tried to hurt Liz."

"Where are you?" Ryan grabbed Shandra's hand, pulling her out of the teepee behind him.

"The parking area behind the Higheagle camp."

"We're coming." He shoved the phone back in his holster and kicked up into a jog.

"What's wrong?" Shandra asked, keeping up with him.

"Someone attacked Liz."

"Oh no! Why?"

"We're going to find out."

Chapter Thirteen

As soon as she saw Logan, Shandra ran forward. Liz sat up against the tire of a vehicle. "Do I need to call an ambulance?"

"No. They knocked the wind out of me and scared me." Liz glared up at Logan. "He won't let me get up."

"You could be hurt worse than you think."

Shandra knelt beside her cousin. "Do you hurt anywhere?"

"Other than my pride? No. Like I said, I just got the wind knocked out of me. If Logan hadn't come looking for me, then I might be needing the EMTs."

"Who did this?" Ryan asked.

"I don't know. I was leaning in my car, putting my regalia away and someone shoved me from the back. I kicked backward and connected with what felt like a shin bone. The person grunted and grabbed my hair. That's when Logan yelled and whoever it was threw me to the ground and ran off." She reached up toward

Logan who grasped her hand and raised her to her feet. He moved in close, giving her his body to lean on.

"Did you see who it was?" Ryan asked Logan.

"It's dark and they were too far away. Someone in a black hoodie that hid their face. But when they ran away, not to sound chauvinistic, but the person ran like a girl."

"You think a woman attacked Liz?" Shandra's gaze drifted between her cousin and her friend. "What woman wouldn't want you talking to Liz?"

"It may not have anything to do with Lucille's death," Liz said. "I've lost a couple of cases the last six months. It could have been someone not happy with the outcomes." She patted Logan's chest. "Can we get out of the parking lot?"

"Yeah, come to our teepee." Shandra grasped Ryan's hand.

"I'll stay here and see if I can find anything the assailant may have dropped." He squeezed Shandra's hand and pulled out his phone, opening the flashlight app.

"Come on then." Shandra led the other two back to the teepee. Inside, in the light, she could see Liz's face was pale and her eyes didn't shine as bright as usual.

"Are you sure you're okay? You don't look well."

"I'm just shaken up. I'm flashing through my cases trying to figure out who would have been this bold." She glanced around. "You don't happen to have any water, do you?"

"I'll get some. Be right back." Logan lowered Liz down on one of the folding chairs and left.

"I thought he'd never leave," Liz said, joking.

"He just cares." Shandra sat on the other chair,

facing her cousin. "Are you sure you don't need to see a doctor?"

"Yeah. It's been a while since I've encountered that much hostility. And it took me by surprise."

Shandra decided to change the subject. "So, you and Logan?"

Liz smiled. "Yeah. Logan came to me about someone who he felt was being treated unjustly and asked if I'd take a look. After that, we kept meeting up and went out to dinner a couple of times. He's so sweet and attentive. But I don't know if our two jobs are a good mix to not put a strain on a marriage."

"I think if you talk about it, you'll be able to deal with it." Shandra knew she had a lot to talk about with Ryan when they went home.

"Yeah, he is a good listener." She glanced at the tent flap. "I wonder what's taking him so long to get water."

~*~

Ryan slowly moved his phone back and forth, allowing the flashlight app to cover small areas at a time as he looked to see if whoever assaulted Liz had left any evidence behind.

"You find anything?" Logan asked, his footsteps crunching across the dried grass.

"Not so far." He sat back on his heels. "Do you think the person you saw running away could have been Marian Lightning?"

"I've been running that over in my mind. I'm not sure. Possibly, but I think the person was shorter."

Ryan stood. "Like Millie?"

"No. Well… I don't know. It was dark and I was trying to find Liz."

"Let's lock this up and look at it in the morning." Ryan checked to make sure the keys weren't in the ignition and picked up what looked like a handbag. "Here, check this for keys before I lock the doors."

Logan shoved his hand in the bag and keys rattled. "Yeah. They're in here."

Ryan hit the lock button and shoved the door shut. He checked the handle. The door was locked. "Let's go see what Liz can tell us about that will."

"I told her I was coming out to get her water. We need to swing by the Higheagle camp and find a bottle." Logan had the handbag over his shoulder like a woman carried it.

Ryan laughed. "You know you are a little big for that accessory."

"Just go grab some water," Logan said, veering off toward the teepee.

Ryan found the cooler where everyone got their drinks, grabbed four bottles of water, and hurried to the teepee. He wondered what line Logan would give for going out for water and coming back with Liz's purse.

"How am I going to get home if you want my car to stay here?" Liz asked as Ryan entered.

"I'll take you home and pick you up in the morning. I can bring you here or I can take you to work." Logan had that smile no one could refuse lighting up his face.

Ryan glanced at Shandra. She had a smile on her face. Always the matchmaker.

"Here." He handed Liz, then Shandra, and last Logan a bottle of water. Since the ladies had the chairs, he sat down on the pads that made up their bed.

"Liz, the reason we wanted to speak to you tonight

has to do with Lucille Lightning's will," Logan said, taking a seat on the ground near the attorney.

"She came to me two weeks ago and asked me to draw up a will. I did and I gave it to her on Friday. She said she wanted to think on it over the weekend and would bring it back—I have copies of it—the following week and sign it in front of witnesses. She never brought it back."

"Then there isn't a will." Shandra glanced at each of them.

Liz nodded. "Correct. Without her signing the will with witnesses, whatever her wishes were, aren't going to happen. It will go to probate and they will look for Geri as the next of kin."

"What about Scott and Millie?" Shandra asked.

"They are out unless Geri is generous." Liz stared at Logan. "Do you think the person who attacked me had something to do with Lucille's will?"

"It could be."

Ryan agreed. "I would say it is more likely, someone is worried you have a copy of the will or one that was signed. I'm not sure if they were just frightening you to tell them or if…"

Logan's face turned stormy. "I think it would be a good idea if you stayed here, at the powwow grounds around your family. There's no telling if this person is waiting for you at your place."

"No one has a place for me to stay here." Liz stood. "Just take me home. We'll figure something out on the way there."

Ryan saw the way Logan's eyebrows rose. He had a pretty good idea how the night was going to turn out.

"Are you sure you feel up to going home?"

Shandra asked.

"She'll be fine. She has a police officer to take care of her," Ryan said, walking to the teepee flap and holding it open for them to leave.

"Talk to you tomorrow," Logan said as he stepped out first, looked around, and reached in for Liz's hand.

When Ryan was sure the two were far enough away they wouldn't hear him, he said, "Don't worry. I have a feeling those two won't be very far from each other tonight."

Shandra glanced at him and smiled. "Good. We need to find Mia and get her to bed. Tomorrow will be busy."

"Okay Lost One Follows Heart." He kissed her. "I like your new name."

"Me too." She grabbed his hand. "Let's go find Mia."

They stepped out of the teepee as hollering and whoops went up in Jo and Martin's teepee.

"What do you think that is?" Shandra asked.

"Let's go find out." Ryan led her over to the teepee and they stepped in. There was barely enough room for them to stand inside the entrance.

Mia and Sandy were in the middle of the circle of grownups and children.

"What are you doing?" Shandra asked.

"We were teaching Mia how to play sticks, but so far she has beaten everyone she plays," Coop said, making his way over to them.

"Where's Jayden?" Ryan asked, noticing the boy wasn't in the teepee.

"He's over at the boy's tent moping. I guess Andy has been staying in the Lightning Beadwork tent and

107

Jayden's not feeling as social without his big cousin." Coop nodded toward the two playing sticks. "I also think he believes he's missing out."

"I'll go free him from that tent. I'd rather have him with us anyway." Ryan backed out of the teepee and then popped his head back in. "You and Mia stay here until I come back with Jayden."

Shandra nodded, smiling and watching Mia.

Ryan knew where the tent had been set up. He walked over there and heard whispering. He wasn't sure if he needed to announce himself, but he figured it was all guys so there shouldn't be a need.

He pulled the flap back and a group of six boys around the age of Jayden jumped back. Ryan marched over and stared at them as Jayden opened his eyes. They had him on the floor, painting his face with charcoal.

"What is going on here? Where are the older boys?" Ryan asked, pulling Jayden up off the ground.

"They were making me a member," Jayden said, standing in front of Ryan.

He scanned the faces of the other boys. From their downcast eyes and drooping shoulders, they may have told Jayden that, but they had been having fun with him. "Get your things. I want you with us."

Jayden started to protest. He must have seen Ryan wasn't messing around. He quickly closed his mouth and gathered his bag of clothes and bedding.

When they walked toward the Higheagle camp, Ryan glanced at Jayden. His face was as animated as it had been during the dancing. Had he pulled him away from some real ritual or was he happy to be joining them as a family?

"When we get to the teepee you might want to clean that black stuff off your face before we go get Shandra and your sister. You wouldn't want to scare them."

"Really? I'm scary looking?" He said it as if it were a good thing.

"Yeah."

The boy slowed his pace. "Can I go scare Andy before I wash it off?"

Ryan grinned. He was willing to join in on a practical joke. "Sure. But I'm coming with you. I might get a good video of him being scared."

Jayden giggled. This was the boyishness he and Shandra had been trying to bring out more in the youth.

Three tents before the Lightning tent, Ryan put a hand on Jayden's arm, motioning for him to go slower. They snuck up to the flap. Ryan pulled out his phone and put it on video mode before he motioned for Jayden to go.

He flung the flap back and jumped in roaring.

Ryan was right behind him videoing.

A woman screamed and Ryan lowered the phone. They'd come upon Andy and Millie making out. She was shoving Andy in between her and Jayden.

The boy was laughing, Andy was glaring, and Ryan was apologizing. "I'm sorry. We didn't know it wasn't Andy alone in here. Jayden wanted to scare him."

"I did too! Did you see the look on his face? And she screamed." Jayden was chortling with glee.

"Not funny, cuz," Andy said, standing and walking toward them. He glared at Ryan then rubbed a finger on the charcoal on Jayden's face. "Who did this?" His anger turned to concern.

"I found half a dozen boys holding him down and putting this on him in the boy's tent. I figured it was some kind of hazing, but Shandra and I had already decided he was staying with us the rest of the week."

Andy's face darkened. "Can you stay here with Millie? I'll be right back." Andy didn't wait for an answer before disappearing out of the tent.

Millie had regained control. "I didn't mean to scream. You just startled me. Looking like that."

Jayden grinned, not realizing how this wasn't a joke anymore.

"Let me clean that up before you scare Shandra and your sister." Millie walked over to a tote and pulled out a package of wet wipes.

Jayden backed away from her.

"It would be a good idea to get that off before anyone else sees it," Ryan said, wondering where Andy had gone and about the expression that had been on his face as he'd left the tent.

While Millie cleaned up Jayden, Ryan decided to do a little more digging. "Where were you after the naming ceremony?"

Millie glanced up at him. "I came back here and changed out of my regalia as soon as the dancing was over. I didn't want it to get dirty. I'm in a competition tomorrow."

Ryan scanned the inside of the tent and spotted the dress, hat, and belt hanging from a tent support. "What did you do after you changed?"

"All done," she said to Jayden and stood, studying Ryan. "Why do you care?"

"Because Liz Piney was attacked after the naming

ceremony. The assailant is believed to be female."

Her eyes widened. "I wouldn't attack anyone. Especially not Liz. She was helping my grandmother with her wishes."

Andy returned. His gaze landed on Jayden. "You look much better cleaned up." He ruffed up the boy's hair. "They won't be bullying you again. It's not the way of our people."

"We were playing," Jayden said, not sounding at all convincing.

"No, they weren't. I had a talk with them. They will all be apologizing to you tomorrow." Andy walked over to Millie.

"Come on, Shandra and your sister are going to wonder what happened to us." Ryan walked to the door of the tent. "Thanks," he tossed at Andy.

The young man nodded.

Walking back to the Higheagle tent, Jayden said, "Those boys won't apologize, not when they think I told on them."

"I'm sure Andy handled it so they will know you didn't snitch." Ryan put a hand on his shoulder. "Did they say why they were doing it?"

"Not really." He shrugged. "I'm used to getting bullied."

"Do they bully you at your school?" This was the first the boy had mentioned this subject.

He shook his head. "Not anymore. Since living with you and Shandra, I don't smell and I have nice clothes." He stopped and looked up at Ryan. "I'm the same as I was before, but now they don't make fun of me."

Ryan put an arm around the boy's shoulders.

"Some people can't see past their own prejudice."

"What does that mean?"

"It means because you were dressed differently and weren't able to clean up as often as they were, they treated you differently when you were just like them, but living a different way. It's just like the custom of Shandra's ancestors for the boys to live in their own home. They reenact this during the powwow to teach the younger generations this tradition, but in real life, it isn't as necessary as it was back when they were all dependent on one another for survival."

"You think they put charcoal on me as a way to show me I was different from them?" Jayden asked.

"It's hard to say why they did it without asking them." Ryan stopped outside the noisy Higheagle tent. "Let's see if your sister is still winning at sticks." He opened the tent flap and found Shandra and Mia in the middle of the circle.

Coop walked over to them. "I think Uncle Lloyd is going to take Mia to the adult sticks game tomorrow night to make money off her."

Ryan glared and Coop laughed. "Kidding. But he is excited at how well she picked up on this game. She's beat everyone she's played."

"I bet I can beat her," Jayden boasted.

Chapter Fourteen

The following morning Shandra couldn't believe how late they all slept in. But then they'd all been up after midnight watching Jayden and Mia battle to see who was the better stick game player. Jayden pouted all the way back to their teepee. While his sister may not be as clever with school work, she had a talent for the Native American game.

Watching the two, sleeping side by side, she smiled. They complimented one another in intelligence and personalities. She wondered if it was because they were twins or just siblings. Not having any of her own brothers and sisters, she could only speculate about Andy and Coop who also had traits that complimented one another. Then there was Ryan and his siblings... They were all so different, but together they did mesh well. This led her to the grandchildren of poor Lucille Lightning.

Talking with Millie yesterday while helping her

run the beadwork booth, she'd learned a lot about the brother and sister and their bond with their grandmother. Shandra found it hard to think either of them would kill the one person in their life who was always there for them. But she had seen Scott's anger when he and the older woman were arguing before her death.

And the woman running away after attacking Liz. Could it have been Scott's wife? She really wanted to meet her.

"Grandmother why haven't you come to me in a dream and helped us?" she whispered, staring up at the smoke hole in the teepee.

"What are you mumbling about?" Ryan asked, rolling and placing an arm over her.

"I don't understand why Grandmother isn't helping us discover who killed poor Lucille." Her frustration hissed in her voice.

"There must be a reason. Come on, it's getting late. I don't understand why we haven't heard movement outside by now." Ryan rose, dressed, and walked to the teepee flap.

"If everyone was up as late as this family, most are probably just waking up like us." Shandra dressed and joined him at the entrance. Only a few older men and women were moving about in the family camps.

Her stomach growled.

"Let's go see what we can find to eat," Ryan grasped her hand and they stepped out of the teepee in time to greet Logan as he walked into camp.

"It looks like everyone had a late night," the big man said, grinning.

"We were up long after midnight watching Jayden

and Mia battle to see who was better at sticks," Shandra said.

"You didn't happen to bring coffee with you, did you?" Ryan asked.

"Grandmother is up at our camp. She has a pot brewing. Come on." Logan led them around two other camps and into the Rider family camp.

"Ahh, my best friend's granddaughter has come to visit," the old woman, who had been Shandra's grandmother's best friend all through school and adulthood, said, motioning to a chair next to her.

"Mrs. Rider, it is a pleasure to see you again." Shandra hugged the woman and sat in the offered chair.

"*Peléy 'áyat kiyé-twikse ku ti'mine.* That is a fine name." The older woman smiled. "Your grandmother is proud."

Shandra studied the woman's line etched face and faded brown eyes. "How is it she isn't coming to me in dreams if she is proud?"

The smile slipped from her lips and her gaze bore into Shandra. "You now have a guardian spirit. You no longer need your grandmother."

"Is that what she has been? My guardian spirit?" Shandra took the cup of coffee Logan offered her and held it in her hands that grew cold thinking she'd never see grandmother in her dreams again. She'd found comfort in the visits, even if they had only been when she was helping Ryan puzzle out a murder.

"I asked Millie where she was last night when Liz was—" Ryan stopped abruptly.

Shandra swung her head around to see Logan glaring at him. He hadn't told his grandmother about Liz's attack. It appeared Logan didn't talk about his job around his grandmother.

"What is this about Liz?" The woman's eyes lit up as she watched her grandson.

"I escorted her home last night," Logan said. The smile in his eyes said, he and Liz had enjoyed his escorting her home.

"You did? That is nice. You two are a perfect couple." His grandmother smiled and waved her hand between Ryan and Shandra. "Just like these two."

"What can you tell us about Lucille Lightning and her grandchildren?" Ryan asked.

Shandra though the woman was going to reprimand him for changing the subject, but Mrs. Rider turned her full attention on him.

"You are not Tribal Police, why do you care?"

"I'm a homicide detective. When there is an unusual death, I'm interested." His gaze didn't falter as the older woman continued to stare at him.

She broke the stare and studied her grandson. "Do you really think one of her grandchildren killed her?"

"We can't rule them out yet. It seems Lucille may have been killed over the will she was having written up by Liz." Logan refilled his grandmother's coffee cup as other members of his family started emerging from tents and teepees.

"I can't see Millie doing such a thing. She loved her grandmother and the traditions she was learning. That girl had turned Lucille's sales around and got her work in galleries. No, I can't see her killing the person who was making the company get noticed." Mrs. Rider took a sip of her drink. "Scott, he can get angry but I don't think he has the stomach to do more than get angry."

"What about his wife?" Shandra asked.

"That one I wouldn't trust."

"Why?" Shandra and Ryan asked at the same time.

"She doesn't care about Scott. If she did, she would come with him to the powwows and join the other women on the reservation who do good things. She keeps to herself. You can't trust someone who never helps others."

Shandra wanted even more to meet this person that no one could say kind words about.

"There you are," Coop strode into the camp. "Mom sent me to find you two. Breakfast is ready and your kids are looking for you."

"Oh!" Shandra shot to her feet. "We stepped out to see where everyone was and then Logan offered us coffee."

"The kids are fine. Sandy is showing them how to make fry bread." Coop smiled at the older woman. "Good morning, Mrs. Rider."

She smiled back. "Good morning to you, Coop. Married life has been good to you."

"Yes, it has."

Ryan stood, handing his and Shandra's coffee cups to Logan. "I'll catch up with you later." He wanted to see if Logan and Liz had discovered anything after talking out what happened and he was curious if the tribal police had done a background check on Marian.

"Come on. Sounds like the kids are making our breakfast," he said, grasping Shandra's hand. "It was a pleasure meeting you, again." Ryan nodded to the woman who Shandra had come and visited twice after learning Mrs. Rider had been her grandmother's best friend.

"It is always good to visit with grandchildren. Come again before the powwow is over."

"We will. I'll bring the twins," Shandra said, giving the woman a one-armed hug before following Ryan back to the Higheagle camp.

"It sounds like Marian may be the person of interest in this investigation," Shandra offered as they walked.

Ryan nodded. He should have known his wife would pick up on that. "I want to see if Logan has done a background check on her. She and Scott haven't been married that long. She could be after the ranch."

They stepped into the camp and Ryan walked over to the table of camp stoves. A large kettle of grease steamed as Sandy placed flat rounds of dough into the hot oil.

Mia hugged first him and then Shandra. "We're making fry bread! Try it."

Ryan hung back as the twins explained the whole process to Shandra.

"You don't want to learn how to make fry bread?" Martin asked, from behind him.

"I like to let Shandra experience her heritage with the kids. They are all so excited about learning new things."

"And you aren't?" Shandra's uncle asked.

"I enjoy watching them. It is refreshing to see joy rather than pain and anger, like I do eighty percent of the time on my job." Ryan walked over to a chair and sat.

"It must be hard to always see the bad in people." Martin took a seat beside him.

"Yes. That's why I enjoy watching my family and

seeing their happiness and innocence." Ryan glanced at Martin. "That was a good thing Aunt Jo did for Shandra."

"What?"

"The naming ceremony. Now she really feels a part of the family and her heritage."

"Jo only helped with the ceremony. It was Shandra who brought it about. She is truly one of us in heart and spirit." Martin stared at Shandra and smiled. "She is a special light."

"I agree there. I'm fortunate she found me. I just wish she'd keep her nose out of my work. It's dangerous." Ryan had tried to keep her out of the homicide cases he'd solved, but her grandmother always came to her in dreams with information that helped the case. He was glad Shandra had been dreamless about this homicide. It wasn't his and he couldn't get all the information to keep her safe.

"She has her guardian spirit now. She will be safe." Martin stood as Shandra walked over with two plates. They held powdered sugar-coated fry bread with a blob of jam on the side.

"Breakfast, thanks to our children." She handed him one and sat in the chair her uncle had vacated.

"Looks good. Are the chefs joining us?" Ryan glanced over at the cook stove where the twins were still helping Sandy as other family members came by and put bread on their plates.

"I think they want to help until everyone has eaten." Shandra pulled a piece off her bread and dipped it in the huckleberry jam.

Ryan did the same. The jam and bread were a good combination. "This is really good. Think they'll make if for us at home?"

Shandra laughed. "I'm sure they'll want to. What were you and Uncle Martin talking about?"

"Kids." He nodded toward the twins. "How they change a person's life."

"That's for sure. I thought I'd help Millie again today. What do you plan to do?"

He didn't miss the way she held a piece of the fry bread halfway between the plate and her mouth waiting for his reply. What he said was important to her. Did she plan to try and join him?

"Look around the vendor booths and see if your uncle or cousins need help with anything."

She narrowed her eyes. "You aren't going to talk to anyone? Like Logan or Scott's wife?"

"If I bump into Logan again, I'll talk to him. As for Scott's wife… I'll leave that up to the officer in charge of the case—Logan." He shoved a large piece of the bread in his mouth to avoid talking.

"Aren't you just a bit curious how the two met and what people think of their marriage?" Shandra asked.

"I am. But it's not my job. I'm on vacation and so are you. Enjoy it." He finished off his breakfast. "I'm going to see if Martin has anything for me to do." He strode away before Shandra could quiz him anymore. He did wonder about Marian Lightning, but it wasn't his place to interview her. However, he could nudge Logan in that direction.

As if someone had heard his thoughts, Logan and Martin Elwood were in a deep discussion when Ryan walked up to them.

"There needs to be more police stationed around the powwow area. I've already asked Chief George to ask the State Police to send us a couple of troopers." Logan spun at Ryan's approach.

"Is this because of the attack on Liz last night?" he asked.

Logan nodded. "Until the person who killed Lucille finds what they are looking for, others are in jeopardy."

"Are you thinking this person will go after Millie or Scott?" Martin shook his head, disbelief widening his eyes and drawing the corners of his smile down.

"Anyone they think may know something." Logan scanned the camp areas. "How many people participating in the powwow would you say might have some idea as to the will or what happened that Lucille didn't get it signed?"

Martin shrugged. "Knowing how generous Lucille was of knowledge about traditions, she could have told anyone who she thought would benefit from her gift to the center. That means half of the people here."

Ryan whistled. "That's a lot of people. The assailant must have started with the first person who might have a copy of the will. But why attack her here? Why not just go to Liz's office and get the paper?"

"I asked Liz the same question. She didn't know the answer either." Logan's eyes grew stormy at the talk about Liz being attacked.

"Did the assailant say anything? Like a threat?" Ryan couldn't figure out what the person had planned to accomplish.

Logan shook his head. "She said she was pushed from behind and her hair grabbed and her head yanked back before I shouted. Then she was shoved to the ground and the person ran off."

"Where is Liz today?" Ryan asked.

"I brought her here, to hang out with her family. She's not to go anywhere alone." Logan peered at Martin.

"I'll make sure of that. I saw her talking to Jo when we walked back here." Martin put a hand on Logan's shoulder. "You two do what you know. I'll make sure the women are all safe. I'll spread the word to the men." The man walked back toward the Higheagle camp.

"He's a good man, but shouldn't you have told him not to say why the women should be watched?" Ryan asked.

"He knows that already. Whoever starts talking about Lucille's will would be a target. He'll see no one says a word."

Chapter Fifteen

Andy escorted Shandra and Millie to the beadwork tent around ten. While Shandra thought he'd suggested walking with them because he planned to stay and help, she began to wonder what was up when he mentioned he had an errand to run and the two needed to stay in the booth together until he returned.

As soon as they had the canopy opened up and the glass cases cleaned, two women walked over.

Millie stepped forward to visit with the women. Shandra picked up the drawing Millie had been working on. The young woman said it was the best she could do to replicate the piece her grandmother was working on for the contract with the prestigious magazine. The intricate design of colors attracted Shandra's artist's eye and aesthetics. It would be a beautiful piece when it was finished.

Millie sat down with a huge smile on her face. "One lady bought a piece I beaded."

Shandra held up the pattern. "I'm sure, given time, you could replicate this just as well as your grandmother."

The smile disappeared on Millie's face. "That's the problem. I don't have all the time I'd like. This piece was to be to them by December so they can use it in several Christmas ads the following year and put it for sale."

Millie moved her finger over the intricate coloring. "That means it really needs to be finished by November. Three months to construct this piece. I'd have to spend all of my time working on it and not making products to sell." She sighed. "That's what was nice about working for Grandmother. She could work on the pieces of art, while I worked on the pieces that sold for less and the marketing."

Shandra felt for the young woman. She was taking over a business that was the heart and soul of the woman who'd died. It was large shoes to fill. "Do you mind if I take a look around at the other vendor booths?"

"Go. I'm fine here by myself. I might even see if I can start on this piece. I know most of the materials are here somewhere." Millie walked into the tent.

Shandra waited until the young woman returned with a small plastic box and sat down, before she walked out of the booth and started browsing the other vendor's wares.

There were a few booths with mass produced inventory and others with one of a kind, beautifully crafted beadwork, leather work, and musical instruments. Shandra smiled walking up to the booth of the man she'd met who made authentic flutes. He'd been a friend of Lucille's.

"Hi. We met the other evening," Shandra said, running her fingers down the smooth wood of a flute. "These are gorgeous."

"Thank you. I handpick the wood I use and make sure it has a good tone." He leaned forward. "Have you learned anything more about Lucille's death?"

"No. Officer Rider is working on it, though. How well did you know Lucille?" Shandra kept her voice low, to keep anyone from listening in.

"We spent many nights talking about family and traditions. She was proud of her granddaughter. She said the girl would be as good at beadwork as her someday. And the grandson. She loved him, but said he made poor choices." He made a sound in his throat. "The main poor choice was marrying a woman he barely knew. Lucille had a young woman picked out for Scott to marry. But he had other ideas."

"The heart knows what the heart wants," Shandra said, studying the man.

He winced. "True. But in the case of Scott, I don't think it was so much his heart as a way to show his grandmother he could make a living off the ranch, by training and boarding horses."

Shandra picked up a flute. "Was Lucille thinking about selling the ranch?"

"Yes. She told me five years ago that the only reason she hadn't sold it already was because it was a good place to raise the grandkids. But now that they were adults and could leave her at any time, she was thinking about selling and moving into town."

"What about the last time you two talked? What did she say about the ranch?" Shandra put the flute down and picked up a wing bone whistle.

"She said Scott and his wife were doing well with the ranch. That if it were just Scott she'd be happy." He pointed to a smaller version of the whistle. "Lucille said she'd be damned if his wife got a hold of the ranch."

"I'll take two of these." Shandra picked up two whistles and paid the man. "Did she say anything to you about a will?"

He looked around. "She had me sign a paper as a witness on Monday night."

Shandra stared at him. "Was it a will?"

"I don't know. I didn't read it, just watched her write her name, then wrote my name where she told me to."

"Were you the only person present when she had you sign?" Shandra's heart was beating. There was a signed will that might have been stolen from the woman's tent.

"Tammy de Fleur. She's a weaver. Her booth is in the covered area for vendors." He pointed to a large canopy on the other side of the arbor.

"Thank you. Can I get your name to tell Officer Rider? I'm sure he'll have questions for you."

The man picked up a business card and handed it to her. *Blackbird Flutes, owner Elias Blackbird.*

"Thank you, Mr. Blackbird. Please don't tell anyone, other than the police, what you told me." Shandra wanted to tell him more, but she knew Ryan would frown on the fact she had discovered information.

"You think her will had something to do with her death?" the man asked.

"It hasn't been ruled out." She smiled at sounding

like Ryan. Then she reprimanded herself. Her plan going forward was to stay out of Ryan's cases, though technically this wasn't his case.

She hurried back to the Lightning Beadwork booth, knowing she'd stayed away too long. She'd call Logan, tell him what she'd learned, and leave talking to the weaver to the professionals.

Hurrying by a beadwork booth, she stopped and stared down at a small medallion hanging from a metal tree, displaying beaded necklaces. It looked a lot like the middle part of the piece Millie was replicating from memory.

"You like something on the tree?" a woman's voice asked.

Shandra glanced up. The woman standing behind the table was in her sixties, given the start of wrinkles in all the places the face aged first. Her hair was black with veins of gray twisting through her braids. Her brown eyes weren't as sparkly as someone younger, but they hadn't taken on the rheumy film of someone older.

"Yes, this medallion. It's stunning. Did you make it?" To mention she'd seen the pattern before would tip the woman off that Shandra knew where it came from.

"Yes. It was something I saw in a dream and thought it had to be brought to life in a medallion." The woman picked up the beaded chain and held it out to Shandra.

"The colors are striking. How much?" Shandra hoped the price wasn't too high.

"A hundred. That took a lot of hours."

Not if she'd stolen the pattern on Tuesday night and this was Friday. "Fifty."

"I put a lot of time into that piece. Seventy-five."

Shandra was pretty sure she didn't have that much cash on her. She didn't want the woman to see her name on her debit card. "I'll have to tell my husband. Can I give you twenty to hold it for me?"

The woman shook her head. "Someone will come along and pay one hundred. I won't hold it."

Shandra pulled out her phone and scrolled down her contacts for Ryan's number.

"Hey, I'm standing at the booth with Millie and Andy and you aren't here," Ryan answered.

"I found something I'd like to buy and I don't have enough cash. Could you meet me at the…" she glanced up at the sign, "…Kitty Kat Beads and Handcrafts booth, about two rows over and five spots down from the arbor?"

"Does this have something to do with Logan's case?"

"Yes, it's beautiful and I thought you could buy it for my anniversary gift." She smiled at the woman behind the table.

"I'll be right there."

The line went silent.

Shandra turned her attention to the woman. "My husband is on his way. I'm sure between the two of us, we'll have seventy-five dollars in cash."

~*~

Ryan hit the end button and stared at Millie. "Is Kitty Kat Beadwork the woman you said was jealous of your grandmother?"

"Yes. Why?"

"Shandra found something there. You two stay put. I'm going to see what she found." Ryan strode away from the booth, heading toward the second row from the arbor. He turned down that row and spotted Shandra standing in front of the booth she'd mentioned.

"Ryan, over here!" she called out, smiling.

He strode up to her, his gaze landing on the beadwork in her hand. "That looks like something you would wear."

"I love it, but I didn't have the seventy-five dollars the artist who made it is asking."

The ingratiating smile his wife gave the woman made him laugh inside. Something the woman said or did had put his usually mild-mannered wife into her get even mode.

"Let me see what I have." He pulled out his wallet and hoped Shandra had a good reason for purchasing a piece of beadwork this expensive. "I have sixty." He held up three twenties.

Shandra handed him the necklace. It was apparent she didn't plan to let the woman get her hands back on it. Shoving her hand in her pocket, she pulled out three fives. "There you go. Seventy-five dollars. Thank you."

"Do you want me to wrap it?" the woman asked.

"No. I'm going to wear it." Shandra slipped the necklace over her head.

The woman's face paled. "That's a special piece. Too fancy for a powwow." She reached out. "Let me wrap it up in a soft doeskin bag."

Shandra's smile grew and that's when Ryan realized his wife had expected this reaction from the woman. "No, I plan to wear it all weekend. It's too pretty to hide in a bag. Thank you." She looped her arm with Ryan's and they walked away.

When they were out of earshot, Shandra said, "Call Logan. We need to make sure she doesn't go anywhere." She held up the medallion. "This is the pattern and colors in the middle of the medallion Lucille was making for the magazine. And if I'm right, this is her handiwork, not the woman's who sold it to me. I tried to get her to sell it cheaper but she said she'd put lots of hours into it. Hah! She stole this."

"We'll know as soon as Millie looks at it." Ryan led Shandra into the Lightning Beadwork Booth.

Millie took one look at the necklace and rushed forward. "Where did you find that? It's Grandmother's medallion she was working on. The one I tried to recreate."

"That's what I thought when I saw it." Shandra took it off and handed it to Millie.

Ryan was on the phone waiting for Logan to answer.

"Rider."

"We have evidence in the Lightning homicide," Ryan said.

"What kind of evidence?" Logan's tone became serious.

Ryan explained what Shandra found and how Millie verified it was her grandmother's work.

"I'll call the officer at the grounds and have him keep an eye on Kitty Waters. I'll be right over to see the evidence."

Shandra stepped up next to Ryan. "Tell Logan I learned that Lucille had two people sign what they think was a will on Monday night."

Ryan stared at his wife. "How?"

She wiggled her fingers. "Just tell him."

He relayed that new bit of information to Logan and ended the conversation. Ryan turned to his wife.

"How did you learn about a signed will?"

"I stopped by the booth of the man Andy had visited with the other night."

"Elias Blackbird?" Andy asked, as he and Millie approached them.

"Yes. He said Lucille came to him on Monday night with Tammy de Fleur and they both signed the paper. But he didn't know what it was, only that Lucille wished them to sign." Shandra held out two whistles. "I stopped at his booth to get these for the twins and the conversation turned to Lucille. I didn't go digging for answers. The same with the necklace. I was walking by and the design caught my eye because I'd been looking at Millie's drawing of the piece before I'd gone exploring."

Ryan shook his head. Leave it to his wife to find answers when she wasn't even trying.

Chapter Sixteen

Logan arrived within thirty minutes of Ryan calling him. Shandra rose from the camp chair she'd been sitting in as he approached the booth.

"What is this about a signed will?" he asked as soon as he was close enough no one outside of the booth could hear.

"You need to talk to this man." She handed him the business card Mr. Blackbird had given her. "He and another vendor, Tammy de Fleur, signed it on Monday night."

He nodded and settled his gaze on Millie. "The beadwork?"

The young woman stood and walked up to him holding the half-finished medallion in her hand. "This was the piece grandmother was working on for the magazine. I have sketches to show you, she only had half the pattern worked. If you look closely…you can see where someone else put an edge around this and made the beaded necklace." Millie reached down and picked up two other necklaces in the case on the table. "This one I made." She held a blue beaded strand up for Logan to examine. "And this one Grandmother made." It was a black, red, and yellow design.

Logan looked them both over. "I can see a bit of difference in the work." He handed them back to Millie.

"Look at this beaded necklace." She handed him the piece Shandra found at Kitty Kat's booth.

"The band is definitely not made by either you or your grandmother. But the design here," he pointed to the crosses around the medallion, "they look like the ones on the necklace your grandmother made."

"Because she did the beading on that part." Shandra picked up the drawing Millie had made of the medallion. "See. This is what Lucille was working on."

Logan nodded as he glanced from the medallion in his hand to the drawing. "I think I need to have some words with Kitty." He turned a sad face Millie's direction. "I'm afraid I'll need to keep this for evidence."

"If it will help find who killed Grandmother, that's okay." Millie ducked her head, and Andy looped an arm around her shoulders.

"Ryan, Shandra, I'll need you to come with me." Logan headed off through the booths.

Shandra grasped Ryan's hand and they followed behind him. It was hard to think the woman would have been dumb enough to sell the piece if she'd killed the person who'd made it. Yet, there had been several of the murders she'd helped Ryan solve that the murderer had done something illogical and that was what got them caught.

A tribal officer stood beside the booth, staring at the woman who'd sold Shandra the necklace. It was evident by the plastic totes pulled out from under the tables the woman had been putting her merchandise away.

"Kitty, I've got some questions I'd like to ask you," Logan said, stepping into the woman's booth.

She sunk down onto one of the folding chairs by her tent. "I don't know why you police are harassing me."

Logan held up the necklace Shandra had purchased from the woman.

Kitty's gaze barely flicked across the medallion before she glared at Shandra. "I knew I shouldn't have sold that piece to you. I told myself you couldn't possibly know where it came from. But then you challenged me when you put it around your neck."

"Because the medallion isn't your work. It's a half-finished piece Lucille Lightning was working on when she was killed." Logan's comment drew the woman's wide-eyed gaze back to him.

"How was I supposed to know it was Lucille's?" the woman said, staring at her hands.

"Anyone who has been to this or any powwow and is also a beader would know this is Lucille's work. Each one of you has your own unique way of beading. A trademark of sorts." Logan slipped the necklace into the breast pocket of his uniform. "Care to tell me how you had the last thing Lucille was working on before her death?"

The woman sputtered for several seconds before forming her words. "I found it."

"Where?" Logan asked.

Shandra could tell by the disbelief on his face he didn't believe the woman any more than she did.

"Down there." She pointed to the end of the vendor booths where Lucille's booth was three rows over.

"When and how?" Logan crossed his arms. His usual smile didn't tip his lips.

"I'm not sure. After I set up my booth on Monday—"

Shandra knew she couldn't have found it on Monday, Lucille was killed Tuesday night. The woman would have been looking for the medallion and Millie would have said something.

Kitty must have noticed how no one was buying her statement. "No, it was Tuesday when I came from visiting with Mildred Sample. I saw it on the ground, picked it up, and figured no one would miss it." She didn't look at anyone. Her gaze was still on her hands.

"What time?" Logan asked.

"It wasn't dark. I could see it on the ground…" Her gaze rose. "Wait, no. My flashlight caught it in the beam."

"Stop lying, Kitty, and tell us the truth. It's going to come out one way or the other." Logan peered down at her, the firm line of his lips giving him an even sterner expression.

"That is the truth." She didn't look up at anyone.

"Jason, go find Mildred Sample and bring her over here. We'll ask her when Kitty left her place."

"She won't remember. She's bad with time," Kitty said, starting to come up out of her chair.

"She's bad with time or you weren't visiting her on Tuesday night?" Logan remained solid as a pine tree in front of the woman.

The woman sunk back into the chair. "I wasn't visiting Mildred. I was at Bingo. I should have been here setting up but I wanted to see if I could win anything."

Logan uncrossed his arms and rested his hands on his duty belt. "Why aren't you telling us the truth about where you got that beadwork?"

"It was sitting on top of one of my boxes when I came back from Bingo."

"But you knew who it belonged to," Shandra blurted out.

The older woman shrugged. "I was going to give it back then heard she'd died and figured it didn't matter if I kept it."

"It matters to her granddaughter." Shandra stepped beside Logan and shoved her fists on her hips. The nerve of the woman trying to pawn someone else's work off as her own.

"No, you weren't surprised that Lucille was dead. I saw you by her tent the morning her body was found. You had a smug expression on your face. You didn't look like someone who planned to give back her medallion." Ryan now stepped forward. He'd been listening to the conversation and could tell the woman was hiding something more than Bingo gambling. She'd been pleased the other woman was dead. Could it have been because she had the necklace and now didn't have to give it back? He didn't think so.

"Why were you at Lucille's tent the morning her body was found?" Logan asked.

"I saw the crowd and went to investigate. I wasn't the only person there." She glared at Ryan.

Vanishing Dream

"No. You are the only person I saw who was delighted at the woman's death." Ryan landed the statement like a fighter landing a jab.

"Jason, take Kitty to the station. We'll finish questioning her there." Logan moved aside so the other officer could grasp the woman by the arm.

"What about my stuff?" she shrieked.

"We'll put it all in your tent after I get a warrant to search everything here, including your vehicle." Logan waved the officer and woman away and pulled out his phone. "Don't touch anything," he told Ryan and Shandra before asking for a judge.

Ryan led his wife away from the booth. "She was hiding something."

"That's what I thought. Logan should be able to get it out of her." Shandra linked her arm with his. "I'm hungry. Let's find the kids and get lunch."

"That sounds like a good idea." He was surprised Shandra was willing to walk away from a possible suspect. He wasn't sure if he was pleased or worried. He glanced back at Logan slowly walking around looking at the items he'd be opening and going through once the warrant came through.

"You want to go back and help Logan?" Shandra asked, stopping, her gaze drifting back to the booth they'd just left.

"It's not my jurisdiction," he said, as his gut told him the woman was hiding something.

"Go help Logan. I'll round up the kids and we'll have lunch." She released his arm.

"You sure? I'm surprised you aren't finding a way to hang around." He peered into her eyes.

"I'm not the professional, you are." She kissed his

137

cheek and headed off between the booths.

He stared after her for several seconds before pivoting and heading back to the booth where Logan sat waiting.

"What are you doing back here?" the tribal officer asked.

"Thought you could use some help digging for the truth." Ryan sat in the chair beside the larger man.

"You didn't believe anything she said either?"

"Nope."

"Let's hope she comes to her senses while sitting at the station." Logan tapped him on the arm with a fist. "Tell me how you and Shandra got the kids while we wait for the warrant."

Chapter Seventeen

Shandra found the twins playing with their cousins. "Either of you want to have lunch with me?" she asked.

"Sure!" they both replied and ran to her.

How she'd not thought of having children in her life was beyond her. She cherished every minute of their rambunctiousness and the smiles they bestowed on her. They may not have been from her body, but they had captured her heart.

"Do you want to grab sandwiches at the camp or see if we can find something interesting to eat?" She waited for their response.

Jayden made a face. "What if I don't like what you pick?"

"Then we'll get you something else." The children had spent most of their life eating canned and frozen food. They were always impressed when she cooked for them without using a can or putting something in the microwave. It also made their lack of having tried very many foods an exploration for Shandra to find them new tastes and experiences.

"I'll try anything!" Mia said, sticking her tongue out at her twin.

"That's not nice to stick your tongue out. We know Jayden is more cautious than you are. And that is why if he doesn't like what we pick, he may get something else." Shandra led them toward the covered food vendors' structures.

"Look over there. Can we go see it?" Jayden asked.

Shandra's gaze followed his pointing finger and she smiled. A vendor was giving a demonstration of his flute. "Sure."

They veered toward the covered vendor area. A small crowd had gathered to listen to the music and the man as he told a story about flute making. The man welcomed everyone into the large covered area for vendors who hadn't brought their own covered booth.

"If you two aren't too hungry we could take a look around in here before we get something to eat," Shandra said to the twins who were both staring at a booth with dreamcatchers and toy bows and arrows. "I guess we'll look around." She wandered behind Jayden and Mia, letting them take in the items, the booths, and the people milling around.

Mia ran over to an area where a woman was weaving a tapestry. Cloth, shawls, scarves, and wall hangings were folded on tables or hanging on a wire wall behind the tables. "Shandra, look at this! It's so pretty."

"It's just clothing," Jayden said, with little interest.

"But your sister and I stood and waited for you to look all you wanted at the cases of knives," Shandra

reminded him. "Let her look all she wants here."
Shandra walked up beside Mia and noticed the business card on the table. Tammy de Fleur.

"Your work is beautiful," Shandra said to the woman working the loom.

She glanced up and smiled. "Thank you. I can see your daughter has an eye for art."

"That she does. How much for this scarf?" Shandra picked up the scarf Mia had been admiring.

The woman stood and walked over to the table, her gaze on Mia. "Tell me what you like about the scarf."

"The colors, the way the animals look like they're dancing." Mia smiled. "It makes me feel happy."

The artist smiled back at her. "That was the purpose for that piece. To bring smiles to the wearer's face. Ten dollars."

"Oh! I'm an artist as well and that is much too low a price for something you put so much love into," Shandra protested.

"If this scarf makes this young lady smile and brings her happiness, my time was well spent."

Shandra paid the ten dollars and handed the scarf to Mia. The child hugged it to her and the grin on her face matched the happiness in her eyes. Shandra would have paid a hundred to see that much happiness on the child's face.

"I will take really good care of this," Mia told the woman.

"I'm sure you will." The artist had a glimmer of a tear in her eyes.

"Are you all right?" Shandra asked.

"Sorry. I lost a good friend the other day. Seeing the joy in your child's eye over something I created made me think of her. She loved bringing that joy to children and adults through our cultural arts."

"You're talking about Lucille Lightning, aren't you?" Shandra asked.

The woman stared at her. "Yes. How did you know?"

Holding out her hand, she said, "I'm Shandra Higheagle Greer. My family, Higheagles and Elwoods, are camped here this week. My husband was the first law enforcement officer on the scene."

"He's a tribal policeman?" the woman scanned the people walking by.

"No. He's a detective in Idaho. We're visiting." Shandra also looked around to see what booth was nearby. She spotted another one with child sized bows, arrows, and toys. "Mia and Jayden, you two can go onto the next booth but don't go any farther. I'll catch up in a few minutes."

Jayden whooped and jogged over to the booth. Mia wrapped the scarf around her neck and sauntered over, standing next to her brother, studying the scarf while he checked out the toys.

"I also spoke with Elias Blackbird. He said the two of you were witnesses to a will for Lucille on Monday night. Is this true?"

The woman nodded. "It was as if she knew something was going to happen to her. The last ten years she'd mentioned maybe twice that she should look into getting a will so the grandkids would be taken care of. Then Monday, as soon as I saw her, she told me to come to her tent at seven because she wanted me to sign as a witness to her will. When I asked her why now, Lucille just said she didn't trust 'her.'"

"Do you know who 'her' is?"

"I don't know for sure, but I'd say her grandson's wife. Lucille hasn't liked the girl from the first time she saw her." Tammy glanced around and leaned closer. "Do you think that's who killed her?"

"The police are looking into it. Did you get to see anything on the will or what she did with it after you both signed?"

"All she showed us was the page we signed. I don't know what she had written up. But I did see her put it in one of the totes. That's all I know." Tammy wandered back to her loom. "Seeing the happiness in your daughter's eyes will help me get through this day. Thank you."

Shandra nodded, glanced at the next booth, and walked over to her children. "Are you two hungry now?"

"Yes!" they said in unison.

"Good. I am, too." Shandra led them out of the covered vendor area and into the food court.

~*~

Ryan and Logan were chatting about the crime rate on the reservation when Logan glanced over Ryan's shoulder and frowned.

A Washington State Police Officer walked toward them with what must have been the warrant in his hand.

"Johnson," Logan said, when the Stater stopped in front of them.

"Rider. I was ordered to bring this to you and help in your search." Johnson said.

The undercurrent of distrust between the two had Ryan wondering what the stater had done to have Logan treating him like one of the suspects.

"This is Detective Ryan Greer. He's going to help as well," Logan said, grasping the warrant and reading.

Johnson gave Ryan the once over. "You just move here?"

"Nope."

"Where do you work?" the stater glanced at Logan. "Idaho."

"Come on, it has everything as I asked. Johnson, since you don't know what we're looking for, you can stand out here and make sure no one walks off with anything while Ryan and I look through the things in the tent." Logan didn't wait for the man's reply, he shoved through the flap on the tent and waited for Ryan to step through.

"We're looking for either the will or something that ties Kitty to the murder," Logan said, starting on the right side of the tent.

Ryan nodded and started on the left side of the tent. They opened totes and bags of beads, looking for anything that might help connect the woman to Lucille Lightning or the murder.

They met at the back of the tent.

"Nothing." Disappointment rang in Logan's voice.

"We haven't gone through the totes out front or her vehicle." Ryan walked to the tent flap.

"Anything?" Johnson asked as they stepped out of the tent.

"Nothing." Logan started on one side of the booth and Ryan the other, going through the totes under the tables and checking out the merchandise on the tables.

"Hey. Take a look at this." Logan held up a crumpled envelope.

Ryan and Johnson walked over and peered at the

paper in the tribal officer's hand.

Dark block letters were written on the outside. KEEP QUIET. THERE WILL BE MORE.

Logan ran a finger inside, then tipped it over his other hand. A small bead fell out.

"That looks like one of the beads on the medallion Lucille was working on," Ryan said.

A grin crept across Logan's face. "I think we have what we need to get Kitty to talk." He faced Johnson. "You'll need to stay here until an officer can be sent over to keep an eye on things while we sort out what, if anything, Kitty had to do with our homicide."

Johnson narrowed his eyes and glared at both of them. "Why is an out of state cop in on a homicide? Does your chief know he's helping?"

"Because he was at the scene of the crime first. And he has good instincts." Logan pivoted and strode away from the booth. Ryan followed.

"Think it's a good idea to jerk around a State Trooper?" Ryan asked.

"I was being nice. He dated my cousin and right after he asked her to marry him, he was out fooling around with someone else. When I told her what I saw, she didn't talk to me for months and said I was lying." Logan spun toward him, anger sparked in his eyes. "I have never lied. Especially not about something like that. Hearts are fragile. Eventually, she heard the same thing from a girlfriend. She broke off the engagement, and he blames me. I don't care if he blames me. At least my cousin won't be marrying a guy who will break her heart after it's harder to get away."

Ryan had liked this officer from his first meeting but the more he knew about him, the more he realized the guy's heart was as big as his broad chest.

They stopped at the Lightning Beadwork booth. He was happy to see Shandra wasn't at the booth. That had to mean she was still hanging around with the kids. This trip had been to help them become even more of a family. Give the children new roots to be proud of. They had met his side of the family and fit right in. Shandra wanted them to accept her side just as easily.

Logan pulled the medallion out of his shirt pocket and placed it on a glass case, then opened the envelope, allowing the bead to slide out. "Millie, can you tell if this is the same type of bead, or if it might have come from the medallion?"

The young woman stepped up to the case and studied the two. "It looks just like the beads used the row before the finish edge. Where did you find it?"

"I'll tell you later. Thanks." Logan slid the bead back in the envelope, placing it and the medallion in his breast pocket. "I'm headed to the station. You want to come along?" He peered at Ryan.

"No. I think I'll go find my family. It's not too much longer until the dancing begins."

Logan's smile slipped. "I think I'm going to miss tonight's competition. I have a feeling my interview will take a while."

"Me, too. But let me know what you learn." Ryan itched to go with Logan, but this wasn't his case. It was his vacation.

Chapter Eighteen

Shandra dropped the twins off back at the area where their cousins were playing after they'd ate and put Mia's new scarf in their teepee. She glanced around the camp and spotted Velma working on someone's regalia.

"Velma, we haven't had time to catch up," Shandra said, taking a chair next to her aunt.

"You have been busy with your new family." The woman glanced up and smiled. "You were supposed to have children."

Shandra studied her aunt. "Why do you say that?"

"Because of how quickly you have bonded with those two. It shows in them and in you." She nodded behind Shandra. "Even your man."

Glancing over her shoulder, Shandra spotted Ryan walking toward the camp. She smiled. He had taken to the children much quicker than she'd expected. "I do believe you are right."

"Humph. I'm always right."

Shandra laughed and rose out of the chair to meet Ryan.

"Where are the twins?" he asked, stopping in front of her.

"Over playing with the other kids. Velma and I were catching up." She lowered her voice. "Did you find anything?"

"Possibly enough to make Kitty talk." Ryan shrugged. "It's up to Logan to do that."

"But you wish it was your case, don't you?" Shandra could tell that while Ryan had sought her out, he wished he were still digging for the truth.

"It isn't and I'm here to spend time with my family." He reached out for her hand. "How much longer until you need to get ready for Grand Entry?"

"A couple more hours." She bit her lip. Did she tell him what she'd learned from Tammy or wait and tell Logan? "Any idea when Logan will be back?"

Ryan peered into her eyes. "What did you find out?"

She told him about her visit with Tammy. "I don't think the person who killed Lucille found it. Why else would they have returned and hurt Andy to look some more or try to intimidate Liz? Tammy said Lucille put it in a tote. We need to ask Millie if her grandmother had said anything to her about a specific tote."

"I should have known you'd seek out the woman before Logan." Ryan didn't say it as a reprimand but more like a fact.

"I hadn't planned on it. The kids saw the flute player, then we ended up in the covered vendor area and Mia loved one of Tammy's scarves." She shrugged.

"Let's go talk to Millie, then I'll call Logan and fill him in." Ryan led her out of the Higheagle camp and down to the Lightning Beadwork booth.

Andy and Millie sat at the back of the booth like an established couple. She was beading and he was on a small laptop.

Walking up to them, Shandra noticed the beadwork was the center of the medallion she'd sketched. Her chest warmed thinking she'd talked the young woman into trying to fill her grandmother's shoes.

Ryan wondered at how well Shandra was digging up clues to this case without her Grandmother's help. Maybe her grandmother hadn't been the one giving her all the clues, but Shandra subconsciously dreaming about them and her grandmother. This was something to contemplate later.

"Millie, we have a couple more questions for you," he said, pulling out a folding chair, opening it, and placing it for Shandra to sit near the younger woman.

"Okay. I've told you all I know." Millie glanced from him to Shandra and back to Ryan.

"You may not realize you know this information," Shandra said. "I talked to Tammy. She and Elias Blackbird were here on Monday night to sign a legal paper for your grandmother."

Millie forgot the beadwork and leaned forward, whispering, "The will?"

"Elias wasn't sure what it was, but Tammy was pretty sure it was a will. She said your grandmother put it in a tote."

Ryan didn't want to let the woman know how important her answer might be. He tried to watch her without looking like he expected anything. "Did your grandmother mention any totes on Monday night?"

"Monday night was chaotic. I'd helped her unload stuff and gone to my family's camp…" Millie stared down at the beadwork in her hands. "I came back over later…She was working on this project." Millie held up the small round she'd started. "She didn't say anything about a tote… but she handed me a beaded bag. Grandmother said she had changed her mind about selling it."

"What did you do with the bag?" Shandra asked. "Did you look in it?"

"No. I knew she'd been back and forth on whether or not to give it to Logan's grandmother as a gift. I didn't think anything about her changing her mind about selling it. I have the purse in the family tent. I put it in with my clothes." Millie placed the beadwork in a small buckskin bag and stood. "I can take you to it now, if you'd like?"

Ryan stood. "That's a good idea." He glanced at his wife. "You stay here and help Andy until Millie returns."

To his surprise she smiled and nodded.

"Let's go." Ryan walked beside Millie. "There's no need to run. If it hasn't been found by now, it's safe."

Millie slowed her pace. "I can't believe I've had it this whole time."

"We don't know that for sure until we look inside the bag." Ryan couldn't think of any other reason the victim would have asked her granddaughter to take the purse back on Monday other than it held the will. But what he wanted to know…did Tammy tell someone that the will was in a tote? It was obvious that was where the killer was looking for the legal papers.

At the camp, Millie introduced him to her mother and grandmother. "We're going to look at something in the tent," she added, motioning for him to follow her into the tent. She walked over to a mattress with a sleeping bag and two bags. One a suitcase and one a duffel.

Grasping the suitcase handle, she pulled it onto the mattress and unzipped it. Millie dug under some clothes and pulled out a beaded bag large enough to hold the folded document. She held the bag out to Ryan.

"You open it."

She pulled it back and flipped the beaded flap over. "There are papers in here." She pulled them out, unfolding the document. "It is the will." Tears glistened in the corners of her eyes.

"Put it back in the purse and put it back in the suitcase. Looks like I'll be visiting with your family until Logan or someone else from the tribal police get here."

Ryan pulled out his phone and dialed Officer Logan Rider.

"How did you know I was just getting ready to go into the interview room?" Logan asked with a touch of humor in his voice.

"I didn't. Figured I'd have to leave a message. We found the will." Ryan went on to explain what Shandra had learned and how they'd asked Millie about her grandmother giving her a tote.

"Take photos of where you found it and then bring it to the police station. I need to get this interview started." Logan ended the call.

"I guess there's been a change of plans," Ryan told

Millie. He set his phone to camera mode and took photos of the suitcase, the bag, the papers in the bag, and then asked if the young woman had anything he could put the bag in to take it to the police station.

She came up with a plastic grocery bag.

"Thanks." He stopped at the teepee flap. "Don't tell anyone about this. Not even your brother."

"Scott didn't kill grandmother," she said emphatically.

"He may not have, but his wife had no love lost for your grandmother or vice versa. Keep this between you and Andy. Because he's going to want to know what we found. Tell Shandra I'll take this to the police station and be back in time for Grand Entry."

"I will."

Ryan ducked out of the teepee, smiled at the older women staring at him, and headed for his vehicle. Even though he and Millie were the only ones who knew what he carried, he didn't want the wrong person to figure it out. He planned to be back to the powwow before his family entered the arbor to dance.

Chapter Nineteen

Shandra and Andy sold several pieces of beadwork while Millie was gone. When the young woman hurried back to the booth, Shandra had to use all of her patience to not ask if they'd found anything. As soon as Millie arrived, a woman came up and started asking questions about a beaded belt.

Shandra listened to Millie's exchange with the woman while she watched the people passing by. One in particular caught her attention. She touched Andy's arm to draw his gaze from the laptop.

"The guy in the long-sleeved denim shirt and camo baseball cap. He's passed here three times since Millie and Ryan left."

Andy scanned the people. "He's passed this booth lots of times the last few days. I remember the cap and his build."

"I wonder who he is?" Shandra grasped the arms of her chair to push up.

"Don't." Andy put a hand on her arm. "I'll text Coop. That guy has seen both of us sitting in here and would be suspicious if we followed him."

He was right, but it didn't help her need to do something.

"Coop's on his way. I took a photo of the guy while I was texting. That way Coop knows who to look for." Andy stood as Millie wrapped the belt in tissue paper and handed it to the woman.

"At the rate things are selling we-I won't have much to pack up and take back to grandmother's work room." Millie took the chair Andy had vacated.

"Do you know this guy?" Andy asked, showing her the photo on his phone.

"No. But I've seen him come by several times. Why?" Millie gave Andy her full attention.

"He's wandered by more than any other person at the powwow. Coop's going to find him and chat him up, see who he is." Andy put a hand on her arm. "Don't worry about it. Did you and Ryan find anything?"

She glanced at Shandra. "He told me only to tell you and not to tell anyone else. But we found the will folded in the purse. Logan asked Ryan to bring it to the station. Ryan said he'd be back in time to watch you and the kids dance."

Shandra nodded. Finding that piece of evidence was Ryan's ticket to get in on the investigation. "I hope he and Logan can get this figured out." She stared out at the people milling about. "Have you and Marian become friends since she married Scott?"

Millie shook her head. "No. Not that I haven't tried. I've always wanted a sister and thought a sister-in-law would be pretty close. Marian doesn't need

154

anyone. Not even Scott, except to have a place for her business." She scrunched up her face. "I think Grandmother asked someone to look into Marian's family."

"Do you remember who?" Shandra asked. That Lucille had hired someone to discover more about her grandson's wife made her think there had to be a reason. Something Lucille had seen or heard.

"I don't know who. If she paid them, it might be in her checkbook or she might have a paper about hiring someone." Millie shrugged.

"Where did she keep her business paperwork?" Shandra asked.

"In her workroom. She has a wooden dresser in the back of the room where she keeps all her paperwork and leather."

"You aren't going there to look around," Andy said before Shandra had even thought about it.

"Ryan and Logan are busy. What if whoever is looking for the will decides to look at the house?" She had promised herself, and Ryan, she'd stay out of this, but he was tied up and she wanted to know all she could about the woman Lucille had misgivings about.

"I can call Scott. He can take you to her workroom and help you look," Millie said, standing.

"No. I don't want anyone to know I'm coming ahead of time. I can say you sent me to pick up something you need here. I'm sure you've told him I've been helping with the booth." Shandra's plan was coming together as she talked.

"You aren't going alone," Andy said. He glanced down at Millie.

His loyalty to her and to his girlfriend was etched

on his face.

"I'll take Velma. Who would think of messing with us?" Shandra knew Velma was always ready to cause someone discomfort. It was her gift.

"I'm not sure…" Andy was staring over her shoulder.

Craning her neck, Shandra looked behind her and spotted the guy in the camo hat coming back around and several people behind him was Coop.

Andy's phone dinged. "Coop says the guy stopped a few minutes at the Kitty Kat Beadwork booth and then moved on, circling around here again. He says when the guy stops somewhere long enough to start up a conversation, he will."

"Tell him to be careful," Shandra stood. "I'm going to get Velma." She glanced down at Millie. "What can I say I'm there to pick up that makes my trip sound reasonable?"

"I need more red and black pony beads." She stood and pointed to a case with the larger beads. "These are pony beads."

Shandra nodded. "I'll text you when I'm headed back. That way you can tell Ryan I went on an errand for you."

Andy shook his head. "This is an errand of your making. He's not going to be happy."

"He will be if I come back with information." Even though she was pretending it was no big deal, her stomach squeezed with the knowledge Ryan would not be happy she'd volunteered to walk into the hornet's nest.

~*~

Ryan sat across the table from Liz Piney. Logan

had called her down to the station after telling Ryan to bring the will. She was reading through it to see if it was the same one she'd written up for the victim.

"This is it, right down to the small bequeath to Logan's grandmother." She glanced at the signatures. "While they aren't notarized, they have a good chance of standing up in court if anyone tries to protest."

"Can you think of any reason Lucille would have chosen to have these two sign without a notary or you present?" Ryan asked.

"Only that she could get it done right away and not have to wait for an appointment with me." Liz replaced all the papers in order. "Something must have happened that she wanted to make sure this would be valid."

"If she saw or heard something that made her think she was in danger; why didn't she go to the police? Or even tell someone?" Ryan didn't understand why the woman would make sure her will was in order but not go to someone for help.

"Maybe she was going on a gut feeling. Would you have listened to her if she'd said she had a feeling someone was out to hurt her?" Liz gave him the same kind of superior look Shandra sometimes flashed.

"No. But how do we find the killer if she didn't have proof?" Ryan leaned back in his chair. They were missing something. Something that would help them find the murderer. "Has anyone done a background check on Marian Lightning?"

Liz shrugged. "I'm not a cop or with the D.A."

"I wonder what Logan is finding out from Kitty Waters." Ryan pulled the will across and started reading it. "What does this mean?" He'd stumbled over a sentence that he didn't understand the meaning.

With his finger on the sentence, he swirled the papers back toward Liz.

"Millie gets the beadwork business, materials, and intellectual properties. That means she can use any of her grandmother's signature patterns and colors." Liz glanced up. "Like the medallion design that her grandmother used to land the magazine contract. She can sign the contract and give them that work without having to redo a contract with the magazine."

That made it seem that having the will signed was a benefit to Millie. That meant she would be eager to know there was a signed copy allowing her to continue business as usual. And took her even further from his list of suspects.

"Thank you for that explanation. Is there anything about the sale of the ranch that would cause anyone to not want the will to be found?" Ryan spun the papers back in front of him and continued to read.

"The will benefits Geri and the center. Scott is the only one who loses."

"And his wife, who has made the place into a horse training facility." The more he learned, the more Ryan believed Scott's wife was behind it.

Logan entered the room. His gaze landed on Liz and he smiled. Then he turned a weary face toward Ryan. "Kitty Waters is as cunning as a coyote. She has told me several different versions of how she came to have the medallion. When I showed her the envelope, she flinched. Then went on to say that was from someone who was getting her eagle feathers to use in her work. She tried to use some excuse that the reason she was told to be quiet was the person giving her the feathers wasn't Native." He snorted. "I'm not sure how

I'm going to break through to her."

"Did you ever do a background check on Marian Lightning?" Ryan asked.

"I asked for one. What does that have to do with anything?"

Ryan shrugged. "Maybe nothing. I just like to know everything about everyone involved. Someone who knew that medallion was worth something had to have used it as payment to Kitty to keep her mouth shut about something. Either she saw who killed Lucille and she asked for the medallion as payment, or the person knew she'd seen something and would see the wealth of the medallion."

"You think Marian knew about the magazine thing and knew Kitty would be interested? But how did they know each other?" Logan glanced from Ryan to Liz and back to Ryan.

"That's where a background check might come in handy."

"I'll go check my desk for the information. Stay put. I'll be right back." This time Logan's gaze was on Liz.

When the tribal officer left the room, Liz asked, "Do you plan on getting back for the grand entry?"

Ryan glanced at his watch and winced. He had fifteen minutes if he planned to make it for the beginning of tonight's dance competition.

Chapter Twenty

The Lightning ranch was impressive. Shandra sat on the passenger side of Velma's 1985 Lincoln Town car. It was an automobile built for a tall, wide-bodied person.

"I can see why Scott wouldn't want to lose this place. But if he loses the ranch, where will Millie live and work on the bead business if the workroom is here?" Shandra had been quizzing her aunt on the family all the way to the ranch.

"Millie doesn't live here. Not since Marian moved in. She lives with her mom and comes out here to work with her grandmother. She would probably find a place in town to do the beadwork." Velma parked in front of a side section of the ranch house. "This is the workroom."

Shandra exited the car and waited for Velma. "Do we just enter or look for Scott or Marian to let them know we're here?"

"Why do you need to enter Grandmother's workroom?" Scott asked, crossing from the barn to the house.

"Millie sent me to get some more red and black pony beads." Shandra nodded to Velma. "My aunt offered to drive me out since I didn't know where you lived."

Scott nodded. He didn't appear the least bit suspicious. "The door's unlocked. Get what Millie needs."

"Thank you." Shandra walked up to the door, turned the knob, and walked in. She ran a hand up and down the wall near the door and found a light switch. Bright light illuminated every inch of the room. "Wow! I guess you need bright light to see to do the beading."

She walked over to the dresser where Millie said the leather and paperwork were kept.

"Can you find the beads while I look in here?" she asked Velma.

The woman was already pulling out drawers on a storage unit on one end of a large wood surface.

Shandra bent, pulling open the bottom drawer of the dresser. It dragged heavy. The weight was due to it being full of papers. She hoped the papers or check book were on the top. She'd hate to have Scott come in and find her digging through this drawer.

A file folder caught her attention. There wasn't another file folder in the drawer, just neat piles of papers. Opening the folder, the words on the statement "For investigative services rendered" popped out at her. A glance at the date said this was the file she'd hoped to find. Shandra shoved the folder in Velma's large purse. "Let's go." She pushed the drawer shut and grabbed the bags of beads from Velma's hands.

"You sure that's it?" Velma asked. The woman had enjoyed their investigations too much the first time Shandra had taken her aunt along to help her find clues.

"I'm pretty sure that folder will tell us a lot." Shandra opened the door and stepped out.

A woman she hadn't met, sat atop a horse beside Velma's car. "Who are you? What are you doing snooping around?"

"We're not snooping. Millie sent us to get some more beads for the booth at the powwow." Shandra walked up to the horse and rider. The horse was sweating as if it had been running for hours or had been worked into a lather from nerves. Seeing the animal's wide frightened eyes, she picked the latter. Anyone who was cruel to animals would be cruel to humans. She'd discovered that over the years.

"If you have the beads then leave. I have people coming to purchase this horse soon."

"Are you going to tell them you whipped it into shape?" Velma asked.

Marian glared at her. "I want you off my property, now!"

Velma put her hands on her hips and glared. "You going to throw me off?"

"Scott!"

"Come on. We have the beads, there's no sense in making a spectacle," Shandra grabbed Velma by an arm and pointed to the car.

They were headed down the driveway when Scott appeared from the barn. Shandra wondered if he had any clue how cruel his wife was, or if he was oblivious because she had cast a spell on him. She'd have to ask

Millie.

As Velma drove back to the powwow grounds, Shandra pulled out the file and read. "It appears Marian ran away from home at fourteen, was in Juvenile Detention for a year, then was lost in the system until she turned twenty. That's when she showed up at endurance races. Her family lives in Seattle, but according to the investigator, they haven't talked to Marian since she ran away at fourteen." Shandra glanced up. "That's sad. What could have been so bad in her life that she ran away from home and hadn't tried to contact them since?" She read some more. "It appears the family is upper middle class. Her mom is a teacher; her dad works in computer technologies. Her mom is Chinook and Dalles. That means she wasn't lying about being Native American. What made her so cruel to animals?"

They were coming up to the powwow grounds. Shandra glanced at her phone. "I have ten minutes to get dressed for the grand entry."

When the car stopped, she hopped out. "Thank you for taking me. Talk to you later. And none of this to anyone." She studied her aunt.

"I know. I can't say anything until you figure it out." Velma pulled her tall, wide frame out of the car and locked the doors.

Shandra smiled at her aunt and ran for the teepee where her family was staying.

"Where have you been?" Aunt Jo asked as Shandra rushed through the opening.

"Velma and I went to the Lightning ranch to get more beads for Millie." She hugged her aunt. "Thank you for helping Mia and Jayden dress. I'll be right out."

When the children had exited, she called her aunt back. "Have you seen Ryan this afternoon?"

"No. I'm sure he'll be here to watch you dance." Aunt Jo ducked out the flap and Shandra dressed quickly.

~*~

Ryan listened as Logan read the highlights of the background check on the victim's granddaughter-in-law.

"Runaway. Juvey. Out of the system until she turned twenty. Worked off and on in the horse industry. Participated in endurance races around the Pacific Northwest, and then married Scott Lightning."

"Any mention of family?" Ryan asked.

"Family is in Seattle. Mother from the Warm Springs Reservation in Oregon." Logan glanced up from the report. "Kitty is from there." He stood. "I'm going to see if she's a relation to Marian." Logan stopped at the door. "You two better get going, you're already late for the grand entry. Liz you don't want to miss your competition."

"What about you?" she asked.

"I have tomorrow afternoon and evening to dance. Go." Logan disappeared out the door.

"Not much we can do around here anyway," Liz said.

Even though it was the truth, Ryan was hesitant to leave.

"Come on, you've already missed your family dancing. You might as well be with them while they watch the competitions." Liz waved for him to follow her to the door.

He walked out of the room, but stopped at the door

of the room where Kitty was being interviewed. This wasn't his investigation. His phone buzzed. Shandra.

Ryan walked down the hall, answering the phone. "I'm on my way."

"We are done for the night. You don't need to hurry back if you can help Logan solve the case."

That's what he loved about his wife. She understood his need to find the truth. "He did just find out that Marian and Kitty are from the same Reservation."

"Warm Springs?" she asked.

"How did you know that?" Now he wondered what his wife had been up to all afternoon.

"Millie told me that Lucille had been suspicious of Marian and had someone look into her background. I found the file at Lucille's workshop at the ranch."

His heart pounded with dread. "You shouldn't have been at the ranch alone."

"I wasn't. Velma went with me. Millie also needed more beads. We got those for her, and I found the file where she said it might be."

"When did the victim receive the information?" He wondered if that was the catalyst for Lucille getting her friends to sign the will.

"The file was signed the middle of last week. She might have received it in the mail Saturday or Monday." Shandra paused. "I wondered where she had it mailed to? Surely not the ranch. It would have raised Marian's suspicions."

"Don't go digging anymore," Ryan said.

"And there is a young man who keeps walking by the bead booth. Coop was following him and said he stopped at Kitty's booth then circled back around to

Millie's booth. He was going to start up a conversation with the guy when he got a chance."

"Shandra, you can't go dragging your family into murder investigations." Ryan groaned.

"Andy took a photo of the guy. I'll have him text it to you. Maybe it will help with questioning Kitty."

He heard her talking to someone else. At least she and the kids weren't alone. They had a large family to keep them safe.

His phone dinged. Opening his email, the side view of a young man appeared. His phone dinged again. This time it was a full front view. There was something familiar about the face and build.

"I received the photos. Did you see the one that is front view?" he asked Shandra.

"No. Why?"

"He looks familiar. Take a look. I'll call you back when I get finished showing this to Logan." He ended the conversation and knocked on the interview room door.

A weary Logan opened the door. "I thought I told you to go back to the powwow."

Ryan held up his phone. "Shandra and her cousins have been sleuthing. This person has been seen multiple times walking past Lucille's booth and stopped as if looking for Kitty at her booth."

Logan's face lit up. "You think this might be our trigger to get her talking?"

"He looks familiar to me. But he shouldn't unless he's been in trouble with the law before."

A big hand captured his phone. Logan stared at it for a long time. "You're right, he does look familiar. Not so much that I've seen him but someone like him."

"Let's hold off on showing this to Kitty until we can name him." Logan popped back into the room and returned with a file. "I'm having them hold her overnight. I hope that gives us time to get a name to that photo."

"Shandra and her family are working on it." Ryan said. "Which means I need to get back to the powwow grounds as soon as possible before one of them finds trouble."

Logan laughed. "Good luck with that!"

Chapter Twenty-one

After talking to Ryan, Shandra asked Coop and Andy if they thought the photo looked like anyone they knew. They agreed he had a familiarity to him but couldn't place it. She and the twins were still dressed in their regalia. She led them back down to the arbor floor, looking for Aunt Jo and Liz. They might have an idea.

On the way, she spotted Logan's grandmother dressed in traditional regalia, sitting in a chair at the edge of the floor. Why she wished to get her grandmother's best friend's praise she didn't know, other than it would be as close to her grandmother's blessing as she could get.

"Let's go talk to Mrs. Rider," she said to the twins as they veered over to the woman.

"Shandra and children. You all look wonderful." Mrs. Rider leaned forward, smiling. "And the two of you did a fine job of dancing."

Mia grinned. "Shandra said I can dance the Jingle

Dance tomorrow afternoon."

"I think that is a good idea. You will do a fine job." The old woman shifted her gaze to Jayden. "You are learning the dance from someone who has been doing it since he was old enough to walk. Logan loves to dance. It's a shame he is missing the competition tonight."

Shandra felt bad that he wasn't here to dance for his grandmother. "He's working on Lucille's death." She held up her phone with the photo of the young man that showed his face. "We all think this person looks familiar but can't figure out why."

Mrs. Rider took the phone and studied the photo. "That is because you have all been close to his family. He is a Lightning."

Shandra stared at the old woman. "What do you mean he is a Lightning? I thought there was only Scott and Millie?"

"Geri is a Lightning. She had two boys. I would say this is one of those boys. He has Scott's build and Millie's eyes."

Shandra retrieved her phone. "Do you know their last name? I would think it would be their father's last name?"

"I don't believe Lucille ever mentioned the father's last name. I think she said the boys' names are Douglas and Nathan." Mrs. Rider studied her. "Does he have something to do with Lucille's death?"

"I don't know. But he is here, at the powwow grounds. He's been passing Lucille's booth several times a day and not making any contact with Millie. He has to know it is his grandmother's booth and he has cousins. Why hasn't he contacted them?" Shandra wasn't really looking for answers. The questions just spilled out of her. "And why hasn't grandmother contacted me to help solve this death?"

Her grandmother's oldest friend grasped Shandra's free hand with both of hers. "You no longer need her. Your wyakin has told you your path."

She peered into the old woman's eyes and felt as if she were peering into her grandmother's eyes.

"There's Ryan!" Mia said.

Shandra shook out of the thought and scanned the area where her daughter pointed. Ryan stood by Andy and Coop on the outside of the dancing area.

"Thank you for the wise words," she said to Mrs. Rider and grabbed the children's hands. They wove their way over to the edge of the arbor below her family.

Ryan knelt down. "Are you still dancing?"

"No. I went looking for Aunt Jo or Liz, but Logan's grandmother identified the person in the photo." She handed Mia up to him and then Jayden.

"Who is it?" Ryan started to grasp her hand to lift her up.

"I'll meet you at the entrance." She headed along the edge of the dancing toward the opening where the dancers entered.

The drum beats grew in volume as the singing faded away. Her feet hit the ground with each beat, moving her closer to the opening. Something pressed her to get to Millie. She didn't know why the young woman would be in danger, but it was as if the drums spoke her name.

Ryan met her at the entrance, pulling her away from the opening and the crowd of people waiting their turn to compete.

"Who is the person in the photo?"

"Come, I'll tell you as we check on Millie." Shandra walked as quickly as she could, her dress jingling with each step. "Mrs. Rider said it is either Douglas or Nathan. Scott and Millie's cousin from their Aunt Geri."

Ryan stopped.

When she kept on walking, he caught back up to her.

"Cousin? And Millie didn't know who he was?" Ryan grabbed her hand, stopping her. "Why wouldn't she know her own cousin?"

"I have a feeling Scott and Millie don't know anything about the cousins. Mrs. Rider didn't even know the last name. She just knew Geri had two boys and that their names were Douglas and Nathan. She made the connection saying the person has Scott's build and Millie's eyes."

"Come on. I have a feeling Millie is in trouble." Shandra started jogging.

Ryan followed.

They both stopped thirty feet from the beadwork booth. Several glass cases had been shattered and the flap to the tent behind the booth was open, revealing things torn up inside.

"Where is Millie?" Shandra pulled out her phone and scrolled to Andy.

"Hey, where did you run off to?" Andy answered.

"Where's Millie?" she asked, not answering his question.

"She should be in line waiting to dance. Why?"

"Make sure that is where she's at and call me back." Shandra couldn't believe the destruction. "If she went to dance there wouldn't be any jewelry inside the cases, so why did someone break them?"

Ryan had taken photos of the outside while she'd talked to Andy. Now he walked toward the tent, taking photos of the inside. "That's documented. Let's see if we can tell if anything is missing."

Shandra followed him into the tent. Her phone rang as Elias Blackbird stuck his head in the tent.

"Is she there?" Shandra asked her cousin.

"Yeah. I'm standing beside her. Why?"

"Someone trashed the booth and the inside of the tent, again. I was worried she'd been here when they did." Shandra waved her hand to Elias to enter the tent.

"We'll be right there." Andy ended the conversation.

"Did you see who did this?" Shandra asked the flute maker.

"I heard noise, sounded like glass, but I wanted to get today's money hidden in my tent before I came looking." He shook his head. "What is this person after? Why be so destructive?"

"This looks as much like frustration and rage as actually hunting for something," Ryan motioned to the tent flap. "You two need to step out of here and don't touch anything outside. I'm going to call Logan. Tell him about this and the info you found out."

Shandra nodded and led Elias out of the tent and outside of the ring of broken glass cases.

"Why would someone do this?" Elias asked, scanning the area of shattered glass and pieces of wood.

"Oh!" Millie lurched forward.

Andy's arm around her kept her from hurdling into the glass.

"Why?" She moaned. "I can't continue to sell without cases and tables. I don't understand who would do this? Or why?"

Ryan walked out of the tent. He'd filled Logan in and was told to keep everyone out of the crime scene. He walked over to Millie. "This is a crime scene."

"Oh no! Was someone else hurt?" Her eyes widened and her voice became screechy.

"No. Thank goodness, no one was hurt. But Logan is sending State Police to check for fingerprints and anything else that might help us figure out who did this." Ryan motioned for Shandra to move closer to the woman.

He walked over to Blackbird. "Tell me exactly what you heard and how long after the noise stopped you came to see what had happened?" He found it interesting the man hadn't run right out to see what was happening if he heard the glass breaking. Ryan glanced at the other tents. It appeared most people were at the arbor either dancing or watching.

"I didn't hear anything until I'd pulled my head…" He stopped and looked around before lowering his voice. "I keep my money in the bottom of a barrel in my tent. My head and arms were down in the thing. I straightened and heard glass shatter. I waited, didn't hear anymore, so I finished putting things back in the barrel and then I came out to look."

"And that's when you entered the tent and found my wife and I?" Ryan asked.

"Yeah. The glass I heard was probably five minutes before I walked into the tent and found you." He scratched his head. "I did stop a bit and stare at the mess. Couldn't believe someone would be this mean."

Ryan kicked himself. He should have regarded Shandra's feeling Millie was in danger more seriously. They might have seen the person who did this.

"Did you see anyone lurking around here when you went to your tent?" Ryan glanced over at Shandra, Millie, and Andy. The cousins were consoling the crying young woman.

"It was pretty quiet, like I'd expected with everyone at the dancing." Blackbird's eyes widened. "There was a young man. I've seen him in this area several times. I don't know if he has a booth or is family of someone who does."

Ryan pulled out his phone and scrolled to find the photo of the Lightning cousin. "Was it this person?"

"That's him. He was standing over there." He pointed to a tent, one down from the Lightning tent. "His back was to me, but I remembered the cap."

"Was he looking at something or trying to avoid being seen?" Ryan asked.

"I don't remember. I just thought, 'that guy's been around here a lot. He must be staying in one of the tents.'"

"Thank you. Go on back to what you were doing." Ryan walked away from the man and over to the trio. "Millie, are you sure you don't know who this person is?" Ryan asked, holding up his phone with the photo visible.

She shook her head. "Only that he walked by the booth many times during the day. Why? Did he do this?" The young woman waved her hands. "Why would anyone do this?"

Ryan wondered if he should bring up her cousin or wait for Logan. It wasn't his investigation even though he kept being pulled into it. He glanced at Shandra. And his wife couldn't seem to stay out of it either. "Andy, stay with Millie until her family gets back from the dancing. Then I want to talk to you and Coop. Shandra and I will wait here until law enforcement shows up."

Andy nodded. "Come on." His arm still remained around Millie's shoulders. "Do you want to go to the dancing or wait for your family to return?"

Ryan didn't hear her answer, but the two headed toward the family camps and not the arbor.

"Did Elias say he saw her cousin here before this happened?" Shandra asked.

Ryan nodded. "Come on, let's see if we can scrounge up some chairs and wait."

Chapter Twenty-two

Coop and Sandy, along with the twins and Fawn, walked up to the vandalized booth. Shandra walked out to meet them. She didn't want the children to see the destruction, knowing she and Andy had been helping in this booth the last few days.

"What happened?" Coop asked.

"Ryan will fill you in. Sandy, will you walk with me and the kids to our teepee?" She was ready to call it a night. She hadn't wanted to hike the jingle dress up to sit while they'd waited. Her feet were tired from standing and her mind just kept spinning in circles. She needed something to take her mind off everything other than the children.

Sandy nodded. Shandra put a hand on Mia and Jayden's shoulders and Sandy held Fawn's hand as they all walked back toward the family camp.

"Did you enjoy watching the dancing?" she asked the kids.

Mia nodded her head vigorously. "Aunt Jo looks so peaceful when she dances."

Shandra smiled. "It is a spiritual thing to dance. Something I hope you learn in the coming years." She glanced at Jayden. "And you? Did you enjoy the dancing?"

"Not so much. I wanted to see Andy and Officer Rider dance." He peered up at her. "Why didn't they dance?"

"Yeah. Why didn't Daddy dance?" Fawn asked.

Her chest squeezed thinking about why the two hadn't made the competition. "Officer Rider is working on a case. Just like when Ryan has a case and we don't see him much. And Andy is trying to help his friend Millie through a tough time. I'm sure they will both be at the competition tomorrow." She hoped this was all solved by then. If the cousin was the cause of everything, all they had to do was find him and see if he'd talk.

Sandy stopped outside the teepee and said quietly, "Can we talk?"

"Let me get these two out of their regalia."

"I'll hand Fawn off to Jo and be right back," Sandy said.

Shandra ducked into the teepee and helped the twins out of their dancing clothes and into pajamas. "You two can read a book until I come back in."

Jayden lay down on Mia's sleeping bag and they opened a book.

Shandra smiled at the two and slipped back out into the growing darkness.

Sandy stood from a chair she was sitting in near the tables used for the camp stoves.

Shandra joined her and sat, drawing the younger woman back down into her chair. "What did you want to talk about?"

"I'm-we're-I don't want anything to happen to Coop," Sandy blurted out.

Shandra faced the woman. "He won't get hurt. He's smart."

"He said you asked him to follow a person today. One he never had a chance to talk with. If the person you had him following is the same one who angrily tore up Millie's booth, then I'm glad he didn't get a chance to talk with him. I don't want something to happen to Coop."

"He doesn't need to follow the person anymore. We think we know who he is. I'm sure once Logan gets here, he'll have the person under arrest in no time." Shandra tried to see Sandy's face in the growing darkness. "I would never put any of my family members in harm."

"Yet, you have put yourself in harm's way many times."

She nodded. "I have. But no more. Once Lucille's murder is solved, I'm not butting into any more of Ryan's cases. The children need me. I want to be the best mother to them as I can be. That means protecting them from all the bad things Ryan sees. The only way to do that is if I stay away from those things as well."

"That's a good idea. When—I mean if Coop and I have children—"

Shandra butted in. "You two are pregnant, aren't you? That's why you're so worried about Coop getting hurt?"

Sandy reached out. "Don't tell anyone. I haven't

178

told Coop yet. I was going to do it this weekend but with everything that has been happening, I haven't found the right moment."

Happiness filled Shandra. For her cousins and her aunt and uncle who would make wonderful grandparents. "There is no need to be afraid of telling Coop. If you've been watching him with the twins, he's a natural father. And he will be happy."

"We hadn't planned on kids yet. I still need to finish one more year of school."

"Then you'll figure out how to make it work. If you haven't learned it already, Higheagles make the best of any situation."

~*~

Ryan and Coop sat in the chairs waiting for Andy to return and Logan, or other law enforcement, to arrive.

"Any idea what is taking so long for a forensic team to get here?" Ryan asked.

"You said it was State Police. They would have to get rounded up and then drive here from Spokane." Coop stretched his long legs out in front of him. "Could take a couple of hours."

Ryan moaned.

Coop laughed. "I bet Logan shows up before the State Police."

"And you'd win the bet." Logan walked up from the side of the booth.

Ryan shot to his feet. "Did you get anything out of the suspect you were interviewing?"

"The information about her and Marian being from the same Reservation made her tongue wiggle a little more." Logan chuckled. "She knew a bit of the young woman's background. Enough that Marian was being blackmailed. That was how Kitty got the medallion. It was a blackmail payoff."

"Are you having the writing on the envelope matched to Marian's?" Ryan asked.

"Soon as we get a sample."

"Do you think Lucille caught Marian stealing the medallion and that's why she was killed?" Coop asked.

Logan shook his head. "We won't know until I get a chance to talk to Marian. I sent an officer out to the ranch to bring her in since I don't have the time to run out there myself and talk with her." He pulled a flashlight off his duty belt and shone it around the destroyed booth. "Whoever did this was mad."

"Because he couldn't find the will, maybe," Ryan offered.

"Could be. But how did he know about it? If, as you believe, he is a grandson from her estranged daughter, how would he even know about the will?" Logan flicked the light beam across Ryan and Coop.

"Guess we need to figure out who he is and where he's staying," Ryan said.

"Who?" Andy asked, joining the group.

"The guy in the photo I took," Coop answered.

"He did this?" Anger deepened Andy's voice.

"We don't know for sure, but Elias Blackbird saw him." Ryan went on to tell the three everything he and Shandra discovered when they hurried here thinking Millie might be in danger.

"I don't think Millie even knows she has cousins," Andy said. "She's never mentioned them. Only her aunt she's never met."

"Don't mention anything we've discussed to

anyone," Logan said as people started wandering back from the dancing. "Ryan, wait with me. You two go on. Andy, don't tell Millie anything. Especially not about the cousin, until we're certain."

"Yes, sir. But it seems like she's the one that's been targeted since her grandmother's death." Andy sounded defensive.

"If she's with her family tonight and you stick by her side during the day, she'll be fine." Logan waved the flashlight beam toward the tent. "Come on, Ryan."

They entered the tent. Logan swung the beam of light slowly over the trashed items in the tent. Beads glittered on the ground. Wire, lace, and string had been strung out.

"This looks deliberate," Logan said.

"That's what I thought." Ryan snapped his fingers. "We didn't ask Millie if she'd left today's proceeds in here before she went to the competition." He pulled out his phone and scrolled the contacts for Andy.

"You need me to come back?" he answered hopefully.

"No. Do you know what Millie did with the money from today's sales?"

"Yeah. It's in her parent's teepee. Why?"

"We were just wondering if that had been the motive. Thanks." Ryan ended the conversation and relayed what he'd learned to the tribal officer.

"If the person who did this was looking for the money, this mess would be a good way to take a while to find out the money was missing. But the smashed cases outside…that could be his frustration at not finding the money." Logan backed out of the doorway and waited for Ryan. "Nothing can be done until forensics arrives."

"What happened here?" a middle-aged man asked, walking up to Logan.

"Someone destroyed this booth about…" Logan glanced at Ryan.

"Nine tonight," he supplied.

"Nine? I'll go ask my wife if she saw anything. She came back to our tent to rest. She's not been feeling well." The man started to walk away.

"Wait a minute." Logan stopped him. "Ryan, hang out here for the forensics team. I'll go talk to his wife."

"I will." Sighing, Ryan found the chair he'd spent a lot of time in this evening and lowered down onto it. If they were lucky, the man's wife would identify the Lightning cousin as someone she saw near the tent and they could have law enforcement looking for him.

Chapter Twenty-three

Shandra had just dozed off when she felt Ryan slide into the sleeping bag beside her. Shaking the drowsiness off, she rolled toward him and whispered, "Did forensics finally arrive?"

"Yeah. Poor Logan looks like he hasn't slept in days." Ryan yawned. "Glad this isn't my case."

"Right. You are just as involved as he is. Did you learn anything new?"

"Another person confirmed the man from the photo was hanging around the tent before we discovered the vandalism. Logan sent an officer to find out all he could about Geri Lightning and her sons." Ryan kissed her. "Go to sleep, there isn't anything else we can do with what's left of tonight."

Shandra lay on her back staring up at the smoke hole in the teepee, listening to her family sleep. Why wasn't grandmother coming to her, helping her discover the truth? Was it as Mrs. Rider said, because she now had her guardian spirit who had told her to watch over her family?

~*~

"Wake up! Wake up!" Mia jumped up and down on the mattress, shaking Shandra awake.

"What are you yelling about?" she asked, raising up on an elbow and looking around.

"Aunt Jo wants your permission to sign me up to dance this afternoon." The child's face glowed with excitement. Her eyes sparkled and her grin spread across her face.

"I thought she already did. What time is it?" She lifted her hand to look at her watch.

"Breakfast time!" The child bounced off the bed and headed to the opening in the teepee.

"Breakfast time," Shandra repeated, throwing back the sleeping bag and sitting up. The numbers on her watch said 8:50. They'd gone to bed late the night before and then her mind had circled everything going on several times, before she'd finally fallen asleep.

Ryan walked into the tent. "Mia said she woke you up. Sorry about that. I didn't realize she'd disappeared."

"I didn't expect you to be up after the long day you put in yesterday," Shandra said, dressing.

"I wanted to know if Logan had learned anything yet."

"And…?"

"Nothing so far. They are looking for the person in the photo and he'd sent an officer to escort Marian to the police station last night."

"He was in no shape to question her. He's been working too many hours to think clearly," Shandra knew Ryan had interviewed potential witnesses on

184

limited sleep and had regretted it later.

Ryan held up a hand. "He didn't get to talk to her. Scott was just getting ready to call the police because she is missing." He raised his eyebrows.

"As in looking guilty?" Shandra hadn't thought the woman would run. She'd seemed too sure of herself.

"Logan and his crew are out at the ranch now, trying to see if they can figure it out." Ryan held out his hand. "Let's go eat."

"You haven't eaten already?" Shandra followed him out of the teepee and over to the table of camp stoves where one aunt flipped pancakes on a large grill and another was manning a grill with sausage and eggs.

"I was waiting for you. Of course, the kids have eaten and disappeared." He pointed to the group of children playing at the edge of the camp.

Coop and Sandy were sitting at a table. Shandra filled a plate and sat with them.

"Good morning. What are your plans for the day?" she asked the two. Who were holding hands and smiling. She had a feeling Sandy had told Coop about the baby.

"We have some errands to run, then we'll be back to watch the dancing competitions." Coop glanced over at her. "Are you dancing in the competition?"

"I haven't made up my mind. I would like to, but I don't think I'm ready."

A hand rested on her shoulder. "You have spoken to your wyakin and you have been named, you are ready to dance." Aunt Jo's confidence in her bolstered her own.

"And I hear you would like to enter Mia into the competition?" Shandra gazed up into her aunt's eyes.

"I think it would help her heal. She is doing well with your family, but she still has sadness deep inside." Aunt Jo sat down beside her and peered into her eyes. "It would be good for both of you."

Shandra understood her aunt meant well. But she wasn't sure about competing. She just wanted to dance. "You may enter Mia. If I dance, it will be just for me, not a competition."

Aunt Jo nodded and turned the conversation to Coop and Sandy.

Ryan stood, holding his phone. She hadn't heard it buzz. Her gaze followed him as he walked to the edge of the camp near the parked cars.

If she could help Ryan and Logan, they could all finish out this week fulfilled. She faced her aunt. "Is there anyone here, at the powwow, who Lucille would have confided in?"

"Mrs. Rider, Logan's grandmother." Aunt Jo studied her. "Why?"

"What about family besides Millie and Scott? Did she have a sister or brother? Cousin?"

"Her cousin Earl is bed-ridden. He's not here at the powwow."

"Where can I find him?"

"He lives in Keller. Two houses down from Uncle Martin's brother Charlie."

Shandra had been to Keller for a barbeque on one of her other trips. Keller was a small community along the Sanpoil River. The Colville Reservation was made up of twelve bands. They were spread out among four towns. Nespelem, where her family lived, Omak to the west, Keller, east of Nespelem, and Inchelium being the farthest east, along the Columbia River. Uncle Martin's mother was of the San Poil band. Over the years as the government added the twelve tribes together, the tribes called themselves Colville after the reservation.

"I can take you," Coop offered.

Sandy frowned.

"I thought you two had errands to run?" Shandra said.

"We can both go with you and run our errands after we get back." He said this while staring at his wife.

She nodded her head.

"Let me tell Ryan he's in charge of the twins for a while." She glanced at her aunt. She had a disapproving droop to her mouth. "I'm just going to talk to Earl. That's it."

She stood and walked over to Ryan.

He ended his conversation. "Looks like they have identified the young man as Nathan Lightning. Geri never married. The boys are from two different fathers. She told the Seattle Police she didn't know where Nathan was."

Shandra could tell he didn't believe that. Why else would a young man who had never met his grandmother or cousins show up now, when the woman was getting a will drawn up. "How do you think Geri learned about the will?"

"I'm sure Logan will be looking into that. But it doesn't make sense why Marian would take off." Ryan stared out at the parking lot.

"I'm going with Sandy and Coop to run some errands. Do you mind keeping an eye on the twins?" She refrained from telling him more. Now that they knew who the young man was for sure, she wanted more than ever to speak with Lucille's cousin. See what she could learn. Because of what they knew, Ryan would be against her going to see the man. But if he was bed-ridden and living with a grown-up child, she wouldn't be walking into trouble. And she'd have Coop and Sandy with her.

"Errands? Here? They have better shopping in Spokane." He studied her.

She whispered in his ear, "They are pregnant and are getting supplies to do some kind of reveal, I think."

"How do you know if no one else does?" His gaze bore into her as if she were one of his suspects. Luckily, she had been questioned by him before she knew him and had survived unscathed.

"Because she confided in me last night while you and Coop were watching the tent. I guess that's why they invited me along." She shrugged.

"To keep you from saying anything? I don't think so. You can keep a secret, but as long as you stay with them and don't wander off alone, I don't see a problem. Logan's going to be busy, so I have nothing to do but hang out with the kids." He sounded hopeful and a bit dejected.

"It will be good for all three of you." She kissed his cheek and headed back to where Coop and Sandy sat visiting with their cousin Skye.

Shandra walked up to the table. "I'll get my purse and we can go."

Coop glanced toward Ryan. "He was good with it?"

"Yes. I'll be right back." Shandra hurried into the teepee to get her purse to keep Ryan and Coop from talking.

~*~

Vanishing Dream

An hour later, Coop parked his car in front of a small single-story house with wood piled to one side of the garage.

"This is where Earl lives?" Shandra asked. "I thought your mom said he lived next to your Uncle Charlie. Wasn't the barbeque out in the trees?"

"That wasn't Charlie's place." Coop pointed to a house behind the one in front of them. "That's Uncle Charlie's house. He's at the powwow. Otherwise, we'd have to go visit him before we left."

"How would he know we were here?" Shandra asked, exiting Coop's economy car.

"Word gets around fast here." He winked, helped Sandy out of the car, and they all walked up to the door.

The sound of a television with the volume up high floated through the screen door. She tried to see into the house around Coop.

He knocked on the screen door, making it bang against the door jamb.

The television volume lowered. "Who is it?" hollered a gravelly voice.

"It's Coop Elwood, my wife, and my cousin."

"Well, come on in!" shouted the voice.

Shandra followed her cousin and his wife into the house, through the small living room with worn furniture, and into what must have been the master bedroom. It wasn't very big, but the door to a bathroom stood open in the corner of the room.

An elderly man wearing sweats and a t-shirt with white braids trailing down his shoulders and chest sat up in the bed, staring at the doorway. His brown skin was wrinkled like a shirt that had been slept in. He squinted at them.

189

"You can't be Martin's boy, you're a man," Earl said, waving a hand toward two folding chairs leaned up against the wall. "I only have two visitors at a time. Young man, you'll have to stand and let the women sit."

Shandra took one of the chairs, unfolded it, and set it beside the bed. "Earl, my name is Shandra Higheagle—"

"You must be Edward's daughter. You look a lot like Minnie." He leaned forward. "What can I do for you?"

She smiled. Her heart, as it always did when her father was mentioned, squeezed with regret she hadn't known him. And the admiration that radiated from people when they talked of her grandmother always filled her with pride.

"I am. Why are you here alone?" she asked, to ease into what she needed to ask. And she wondered if he'd heard of his cousin's death.

"My daughter went to the store. She leaves me alone from time to time. It's good for both of us." He glanced at Sandy sitting on the chair by the wall. "You must be Cooper's wife. Pleased to meet you." His gaze came back to Shandra. "Why did you come to see me?"

She glanced at Coop, who nodded his head, then she started with Lucille's death and ended with a question. "What can you tell us about Geri and her boys? How did Lucille know she had the two children?"

Earl used a handkerchief to swipe his nose. "Lucille would come see me once a month, like clockwork. We talked about family and people we knew. There are getting to be fewer of us that grew up

190

together." He motioned with a finger to a glass of water on the bedside table.

Shandra handed it to him. She'd learned from reconnecting with her Nez Perce family that allowing the other person to tell their story in their own way usually got your answers quicker than trying to pull it out of them.

After swallowing a couple of times, he held the glass in his hands and continued. "When Geri first left, Lucille was happy her daughter had found a life off the reservation. Then she visited Geri in Seattle when she was there for a beading event and discovered Geri was dancing at a men's club. That's when Lucille told her to come back to the reservation and learn beading. That didn't happen. Geri wrote to her both times the boys were born, asking for money but refusing to leave Seattle. Lucille didn't send money. She hadn't established herself as a jewelry maker yet and barely had enough to feed and clothe Tom's kids. She told Geri to get a good job and take care of her children herself. After that, Lucille didn't talk about Geri or the boys when she came to visit. Only how well Millie was taking to beading and that Scott was putting the ranch into shape." He shuddered. "But she didn't like Scott's wife. Said she was sneaky and didn't love Scott."

Shandra grasped onto the last statement. "How did she know Marian doesn't love Scott?"

"Because everything Marian did was for herself. According to Lucille, Scott waited on Marian and took care of the house and outside chores while Marian tortured horses." He shrugged. "I never met the woman. She and Scott married elsewhere and then showed up here to live on the ranch with a trailer load of horses."

He flipped a hand. "According to Lucille. I don't get out, so I have only her word to go by. And that of Millie. She comes now and then to hear stories about her father."

"Millie complains about Marian, too?" Shandra asked. She already knew what Millie thought but wondered if it was different when talking to a relative.

He nodded. "She hasn't liked the woman since first laying eyes on her. Millie said the woman is mean to animals and her brother. She said she even showed disrespect to Lucille, which angered Millie even more. She has always been a polite young woman. I can imagine it was hard for her not to say something to Marian if she were being disrespectful to Lucille."

Shandra nodded. She didn't think there was more to learn here. "Thank you for your time. I appreciate you visiting with us."

She stood and glanced at Coop. His brow was furrowed as though he were thinking hard about something.

She elbowed her cousin as she folded up the chair and replaced it against the wall along with the one Sandy had sat on.

"Yeah, thanks for seeing us. My folks say they'll get down here again one of these days."

"I would appreciate a visit from anyone. It gets lonely day after day looking at these walls."

"I'll tell them," Coop said, escorting Sandy out of the room and the house.

Shandra followed them. When they were all settled in the car, she asked, "What were you thinking about in there?"

"Geri is living in Seattle and that's where Marian

came from. I know it's a big city, but do you think the son that is here knows Marian?" Coop backed the car up and headed out of Keller.

"That's a good question." She texted Ryan, asking him about a coincidence that Nathan Lightning and Marian Lightning might know one another from Seattle.

Chapter Twenty-four

Ryan sat near the stick game area watching the twins play with the other children. They'd spent the first hour walking around, looking at the booths. Jayden had led him to the booth with the bows and arrows Shandra had told him about. He knew the boy wanted the toy, but he was more inclined to get him a youth set that he could actually shoot at a target and learn skills.

His phone vibrated. Shandra texted him.

Has anyone looked into whether or not Nathan and Marian know one another?

He wondered where this came from since she was helping Coop and Sandy buy supplies for something. But he had also wondered if there was a connection between them. Logan hadn't contacted him. He didn't know if that meant the tribal officer was still working the case or finally getting some shut eye.

He forwarded the text to Logan.

Barely a minute passed and his phone vibrated.

That is being checked on now. Could use a refreshed mind to help.

Where are you?

Lightning Ranch.

Be there in fifteen.

Ryan walked over to the Higheagle camp and spotted Jo walking with other family members. He walked up to the group. "Could I talk to you for a minute?"

She left the group and stopped in front of him. "Yes?"

"I don't know when Shandra will get back, but Logan called and needs my help. Can you watch the twins for a bit?" He hated asking so much of Shandra's family. They came here to have their first family vacation and it seemed like they had left the kids in the care of Shandra's family more than they'd spent time with them.

Jo put a hand on his arm. "They will be fine. We will keep an eye on them. Help Logan so we can all feel safer."

"Thank you! I'll hurry back and let Shandra know she needs to get back here soon." He headed back to the kids to let them know he would be gone and Jo would be watching them.

"Why do you have to go?" Mia asked.

"Because I was asked to help. If you had a friend who needed help, you would help them." He studied the two. They had had very few friends in their short lives due to their family situation. He hoped that now they were living in a stable environment they would feel more open to having friends.

"I guess. Will you be back for my dance?" Mia

stared up at him with hope glistening in her eyes.

"I wouldn't miss it." He kissed the top of her head and squeezed Jayden's shoulder. "Shandra should be back soon, and I'll be here for the dance competition, I promise."

They both nodded and went back to play.

Ryan strode to the Jeep and headed to the Lightning Ranch. He didn't understand what they were still doing there. If Marian had left, they should have a BOLO out on her and whatever vehicle she took.

~*~

Shandra thanked Coop and Sandy for taking her to Keller and hurried off to find Ryan and the kids. She discovered the children sitting at a table eating sandwiches with Aunt Jo.

"Where's Ryan?" she asked, sitting down beside Jayden and stealing a potato chip.

"He said Logan asked for his help and asked me to watch these two." Jo smiled and pushed a strand of Mia's wayward hair out of her face.

"Did he say where he went and how long he'd be gone?" She knew when a murder investigation was ongoing there was no way to know any of that, but hoped he would make it back for the competitions.

"He told me he'd be back to watch me dance," Mia said, smiling.

"Then that is when we'll see him." Shandra grinned at the child and glanced at her aunt. The woman was deep in thought.

Shandra stood and motioned for her aunt to follow her. "I'm going to get something to eat. I'll be right back."

Aunt Jo said something to Mia that made her laugh

and joined Shandra at the table with sandwich fixings.

"I visited Lucille's cousin Earl this morning," she said, picking up a slice of bread.

"Why did you do that?"

"I wanted to learn more about Geri and her boys. Turns out she never married. And she has worked in an unstable industry all these years. Not sure what she's doing now." Shandra went on to tell her aunt all she'd learned. "I think one or both of the boys learned their grandmother was making out a will that gave them less and decided to make sure it didn't happen."

"That's terrible. How could a child kill their own grandmother?" The horror of it rang in her aunt's voice.

"I don't like thinking that but who else could it have been? And now Marian's missing." Shandra placed a slice of bread on the peanut butter she'd spread on the one in her palm.

"Missing? As in she left or something happened to her?" Fear crept into Aunt Jo's words.

"I don't know. But I'm thinking the latter if Logan wanted Ryan's help."

~*~

Logan met Ryan at the front of the barn at the Lightning Ranch.

"I take it there is a reason you asked me to come out here and we're at the barn," Ryan said, noting the two tribal vehicles, a state trooper vehicle, and an unmarked FBI rig.

"It appears there was a struggle in the barn and Marian is missing. There is some blood but not enough to think someone may have been killed. Yet."

Ryan stared into Logan's eyes. It was evident he didn't think Marian went of her own will. "Okay. Do you have Search and Rescue checking the property?"

"They started out at daylight. This is the command center." Logan walked toward the barn.

"Where's Scott?" Ryan hoped he wasn't out with Search and Rescue.

"He's in the barn. Worried. But he hasn't called his sister yet. He said he didn't want to put any more trouble on her. He knew about the vandalism at the beadwork booth." Logan opened the barn door and Ryan entered, his eyes adjusting to the darker interior.

A tribal policeman sat at a table with a radio set up. A man in a suit, the FBI agent, stood over by a map on a wall. Scott paced back and forth. Ryan could see why Logan needed help if this was all they had at the command center for the search.

"Are any vehicles missing?" he asked.

"No. And all the horses are accounted for." Logan glanced at Scott.

The husband to the missing woman strode over. "This is all your wife's fault. Why couldn't she have kept her nose out of things."

Ryan stared at the distraught man. "What are you talking about? My wife doesn't have anything to do with your wife's disappearance."

"She came here and took papers. Papers that upset Marian. She called someone and now she's missing." Scott pointed a finger at Ryan. "She shouldn't have meddled."

Logan moved between Scott and Ryan. "Go back to pacing. Those papers had information your grandmother asked a private investigator to find on your wife. A woman who has told very few people the truth."

When the man walked away, Logan picked up a file and handed it to Ryan. "Read this."

Before he opened the file, the FBI agent walked over. "Who's this?"

"Detective Ryan Greer. He's here to consult," Logan said. "Ryan, this is Special Agent Wheeler of the Bureau."

Ryan shook hands, glad it wasn't the agent he'd bumped heads with when Coop was a suspect in a homicide and the one who let leak Ryan's true identity to people from his undercover days.

"Looks to me like the woman realized we were onto her killing the old woman and hightailed it," Agent Wheeler said loud enough for Scott to hear.

"We won't know anything until we find her and hear her story." Ryan walked away and opened the folder. He read through the reports from the Seattle P.D. on Marian and Nathan Lightning. They'd both been in the same foster home for a bit, then were both in Juvey for a robbery they'd attempted. It seemed they were partners in crime. Nathan must have told Marian about his grandmother having a ranch here. She made friends and then married Nathan's cousin in hopes of getting the ranch. When it looked like Scott wouldn't get the full ranch, only Nathan's mother if a will wasn't made, the two must have conspired to get rid of Lucille before the will was signed. Only they didn't know a version had been signed until it was too late.

"You think the two, Nathan and Marian, fought and maybe she didn't want to be a part of whatever he had planned anymore and he kidnapped her to keep her from talking?" Ryan asked Logan when the tribal officer walked over to where he stood.

"That's what it looks like. Or Marian got away from him and is out there somewhere hiding." Logan glanced over at Scott. "Whichever, he's a mess."

"Do you think having Millie here would help him? She doesn't have a booth or items to sell anymore." Ryan knew that sometimes it helped to overhear things if the person you were concerned about had someone to converse with that they trusted.

"Give Andy a call and see if he can bring her here. If she wants to come. There was no love loss between Millie and Marian." Logan plucked the file from Ryan's hands.

"That's what Shandra discovered. Could be why the booth has been targeted with so much vandalism." Ryan pulled out his phone and scrolled his contacts for Andy's number.

"Hey, Ryan, it's getting close to time for the dancing to start," Andy answered.

"Yeah, I'm going to have to tell Shandra I won't make it. Any chance you can bring Millie out to the ranch?"

"Lightning Ranch? Why?"

"Marian's missing and Scott could use some support." Ryan hoped the two didn't rush out here and get in a wreck.

"I'll go find her. She was dressing, getting ready for the competition. I'll let you know when we're on our way. You want me to tell Shandra what's going on?"

"I'll call and tell her I'm not going to make the competition. Logan is short policemen."

"Okay. Text you when we leave."

The connection ended. He hit the quick dial button

for Shandra and waited as it rang several times. She was most likely dressed and waiting for the grand entry, which meant her phone was in the teepee. When it asked to leave a message, he told her all he knew and that he'd try to get there for the seven o'clock competition.

Chapter Twenty-five

A group of Higheagle women stood together at the entrance to the arbor waiting for the grand entry to begin. Shandra caught sight of Andy pushing through the crowd of dancers. He stopped by Millie. They talked and the two pushed back through the crowd.

She wondered what that was about. Could it be they'd found Marian? A tug on her dress pulled her attention down to her daughter standing beside her.

"When do we get to go in?" Mia asked.

"Soon. They are calling in the flag bearers right now." The speakers set up inside and outside the arbor announced the presentation of the flags.

She straightened and spotted the camouflage hat that Nathan wore, just above the heads of a group of people seated outside the arbor. Shandra turned to Aunt Jo. "I'll be right back."

"Where are you going?" her aunt called as Shandra pushed out through the waiting dancers. Once she stood in front of the group seated in chairs, she scanned the area in the direction the man had walked.

He ducked between the vendor tents and booths west of the arbor. She wondered if he was heading to the parking area. If he was, she could get a look at his vehicle and hopefully his license plate.

Shandra hurried as fast as she could in the jingle dress without making too much noise. From what she could tell, he was headed toward the parking area. She picked up her speed, wishing she could veer one way or the other so he wouldn't see her if he happened to look behind him.

As if her thoughts telegraphed to him, he glanced over his shoulder. The glare she'd seen in the dark the night Lucille had died peered at her again. She stopped in her tracks and spun around, running back the way she'd come. This time at full speed and not caring if her dress made noise. In fact, she'd prefer that it did to catch the attention of someone.

She didn't hear feet pounding behind her. A quick glance over her shoulder proved she wasn't being chased. Slowing, she stopped, sucked in air, and peered behind her. Had he continued on to his vehicle? Her fear of his harming her had stopped her from getting information Ryan and Logan could use.

Walking down the length of booths, she wondered what he'd been doing at the powwow grounds. Her feet took her to the vandalized Lightning Beadwork booth. Someone, probably Andy and Millie, had cleaned up the glass and broken wood. There was one small case that had been spared. It sat to the right side of the tent opening. Her heart went out to Millie for the loss of her grandmother and the savage attack on the thing she and her grandmother had shared.

Shandra reached up to grasp the flap on the tent and have a look. The flap flew up and a short, slender woman, older than Aunt Jo with her hair braided and pinned on her head, gasped.

"Who are you?" the woman asked as Shandra asked, "What are you doing in this tent?"

They stared at one another for several seconds before a hand grabbed Shandra's arm, yanking her away from the tent opening.

"This is the woman who keeps showing up."

At the voice, Shandra turned her head and cringed. It was Nathan Lightning. Who was the woman?

"She's seen me. We'll have to take her with us," the woman said, stepping out and scanning the area. "Go straight to the car."

Shandra opened her mouth to shout and the woman shoved a cloth in her mouth.

"Quickly, before someone sees," the woman hissed.

Struggling against the young man's grip and trying to kick backward at his shins while he propelled her forward, made their forward motion slower. Unfortunately, they weren't seen by anyone and he shoved her into the backseat of a small economy car. The woman slid in beside her, holding her down as the young man slipped in behind the steering wheel and shot out of the parking lot.

"Slow down! You don't want to attract attention," the woman said.

Shandra rubbed her face back and forth, extracting the cloth from her mouth. "Who are you?"

"It's better for you if you don't know." The woman

shoved the cloth back into her mouth.

~*~

Logan ended his conversation on his phone and walked over to Ryan. "According to the Seattle Police they can't find Geri Lightning anywhere. She hasn't shown up for work all week and her neighbors haven't seen her or the son who lives with her."

"Nathan?" Ryan asked.

"That's the one."

The radio crackled. They walked over to stand behind the officer in charge of the radio.

"We found what looks like a faint trail of someone in boots headed north. Should catch up to them before dark, Over."

"Copy," the officer said.

"What's north of the Lightning Ranch?" Ryan asked.

"The highway. I would say it's Marian trying to get to the highway for help. I'll get someone out there to watch the road." Logan raised his phone to his ear.

Ryan walked over to where the FBI agent was talking on his phone while standing near the maps. The man hadn't put in any effort to help look for the woman. At least not that Ryan could tell.

He walked up to the map, found the ranch, and studied the area north. It was true the person could be headed for the highway and either for help or a way to get out of here. He studied it some more.

"Hey, Logan!" he called to the tribal officer.

"Yeah?" Logan walked over.

"What's this?" He put his finger on what looked like a shack on the map.

"I think it's an old hunting shack. Lucille's

Paty Jager

husband built it years ago. I'm surprised it's still standing." The light went on as soon as the words came out.

"Come on. I know how to get there with horses." Logan headed for the door. "Scott, come help us saddle up horses."

The young man hurried to the door. "Can I go? It's my wife we're looking for."

"I can have a copter over that area in thirty minutes," Agent Wheeler said.

"We're going in on horseback. Quieter." Logan moved Scott out the door.

Ryan's phone rang. He answered it as the three walked to the corral. "Hello?"

"It's Jo. Shandra can't be found. We were standing in line for the grand entry when she saw something and asked me to take the kids in for Grand Entry. When we came out, I couldn't find her. Andy took off with Millie for the ranch. Coop and Sandy have been looking everywhere."

"Keep calm. Don't let the kids know if they don't know already. I'll get there as soon as I can." He ended the call as Andy drove in.

Millie was out of the car before the vehicle came to a complete stop. "What's happened?" She stood in front of her brother.

"Someone attacked Marian and now she's missing. Logan thinks she might be at the old hunting shack," Scott said, as he continued toward the corral.

Logan dropped back to walk alongside Millie. "I don't want Scott to go with us. We don't know what we're going to find. It's going to be up to you to keep him here. Can you do that?"

She nodded. "I'll do my best."

"Good girl."

Ryan had second thoughts about heading out to the hunting shack. His wife was missing and he shouldn't be in the woods when she was last seen at the powwow grounds. "Damn!"

"What's wrong?" Andy asked, trailing along behind them.

"Your mom just called. Shandra's missing." He filled Logan, Andy, and Millie in on what Jo had said.

"She must have seen something and followed the person," Andy said.

That only made Ryan's gut twist even harder. "She knows not to put herself in danger. She has the kids to think about now."

Scott pulled three horses out of the corral.

"Let Logan and Ryan take care of this. The person out there could be whoever attacked Marian. You don't know how to deal with those kinds of people," Millie said.

While the siblings argued, Logan and Ryan found saddles and tacked up the horses. Millie had her brother out of sight as they mounted the horses and headed at a trot out through the trees.

If this had been any other circumstance, Ryan would have enjoyed the ride. He and Shandra rode nearly every weekend. But knowing she was missing and there was the possibility they would be coming upon a hostile person at the shack, he couldn't relax and enjoy the ride.

Chapter Twenty-six

The car bounced over a rough road. Shandra calculated they were north of Nespelem and had taken a dirt road headed west. Listening to her captors, she'd deduced the woman was Geri. It made Shandra's heart ache to think the woman may have killed her own mother. And for what? A piece of land.

"There's the shack. We'll dump her and get out of here so turn the car facing out," Geri ordered.

"What about Marian? They have to have found her body by now," Nathan said.

"It doesn't matter, we'll be long gone."

The car stopped. Geri jerked Shandra to a sitting position and then pulled her out of the car. While they were driving, the woman had bound Shandra's hands behind her back.

Once her feet hit the ground, she tried to run but the woman grabbed her tied hands, pulling her off balance. Her dress jingled as she hit the ground.

"Get her up and into the shack," Geri ordered her son.

Rough hands helped her to her feet and shoved her through the open shack door.

Geri stood in the middle of the room staring behind the open door. The door slammed shut.

Marian stepped forward with a shotgun in her hands. "How stupid can two people get?" she said, sarcastically. "That woman is the one who has caused all the problems for us and you bring her here?"

"I thought you said she'd been taken care of?" Geri glared at her son.

"I thought she was dead. She fell to the floor and didn't look like she was breathing." He scowled at Marian.

"You didn't check?" Geri and Nathan were facing one another.

Shandra edged away from the two. It would be harder for Marian to shoot all of them if they were spread out.

"Stop!" Marian shouted, pointing the shotgun at Shandra and glaring at the two in the middle of the shack.

Fear crept up Shandra's back. She couldn't get shot and be left here. No one would know to look here. It was several months until hunting season. She wished Grandmother would come to her, help her figure out what to do. But Ella had vanished from her dreams. Depending on who survived, they would be long gone, and no one would know there were bodies here.

"Their arguing is annoying," Shandra said, as if that was a good reason to move away from them.

"I can fix them not being annoying anymore."

Paty Jager

Marian pointed the shotgun at the mother and son.

"You shoot us and you'll never be able to settle down and raise horses," Geri said. She was the only one who had a cool head. Nathan looked sick.

Shandra wasn't surprised he'd failed in his attempt to kill Marian. The woman would not have hesitated to kill him if she'd had the chance. Like now.

"With you two gone, Scott could inherit two thirds of the ranch."

"Aren't you forgetting Geri's other son?" Shandra said, drawing the rifle barrel and Marian's glare her direction.

"He died in a shooting a year ago," Marian said. "Nathan told me all about it."

"Did Nathan also tell you that his mother was set to inherit the ranch? I'm surprised you didn't marry him instead of Scott."

Marian's gaze flicked to Nathan. "He doesn't know anything about horses, and he couldn't kill me, what kind of a man can't do a job he's sent to do?"

"Scott wouldn't have been able to kill for you," Shandra said.

"No, but he believes everything I tell him."

The 'cat that ate the mouse' grin that settled on her lips sent a shiver up Shandra's spine. She wondered what Marian's husband had believed that may put him in danger.

"How are you going to explain three bodies in the hunting shack and you gone?" Shandra eased a little closer to the door as Marian stared at the woman and son. She was sure Nathan wasn't going to be much help unless told what to do. And that would give their captor notice of what was about to happen. She caught Geri's attention and tipped her head slightly toward Marian.

"You don't really think you're going to get away with this? You're the only one who has killed anyone. You should get going while you can." Geri put space between herself and Nathan, to the opposite side Shandra was creeping.

A horse nickered.

Marian swung the shotgun toward the door.

Shandra put her head down and rammed into the woman.

Boom! The blast echoed in the small shack.

Shandra landed on top of Marian. The woman scrambled and clawed out from under her.

"Don't move or I'll shoot you," Geri said in a menacing voice.

"Throw out your weapon."

Warm tears of relief filled Shandra's eyes at the sound of Logan's voice. "You can come in!" she called out.

The door, full of holes from the shotgun blast, slowly opened. Logan stepped in. He hurried across the small space and took the shotgun from Geri.

Shandra was trying to sit up when strong hands she knew well, helped her.

"How did you get here?" Ryan asked.

"It's a long story." When her hands were untied, she walked over to Logan. "These three were in on stopping the will. These two are Geri and Nathan Lightning. They kidnapped me from the powwow thinking I knew more than I did."

Geri thumped Nathan on the head.

"Marian was here when we arrived. It sounds like she killed Lucille, going farther than these two had planned to get their hands on the will." Shandra walked over to Ryan. "I'd like to get back to the children."

"You can take one of the horses and head south. The horse should know the way to go. I'll stay here with Logan until a car comes to pick them up." Ryan glanced over at Logan. "If that's okay with you?"

"Sounds good to me." The tribal officer latched handcuffs on Marian.

Ryan walked Shandra out of the shack and helped her onto the horse. "You sure you don't want to wait for a ride?"

"You know me. Riding on a horse will help me clear my head and be ready for the children when I get back." Shandra leaned down and kissed Ryan. "Call Aunt Jo and tell her you found me. I'm sure that's who told you I was missing."

"As usual, you are correct. I'll call Andy and tell him to be looking for you. He and Millie are at the ranch." Ryan watched as Shandra turned the horse south and rode into the trees. Since her seeing the person slinking around the tents that first night, he could finally feel she wasn't in danger.

He walked into the shack and found all three suspects sitting on the floor.

Logan leaned against the wall talking on his cell phone. Ending the call, he grinned at Ryan. "We found your wife and the person we were looking for."

Ryan snorted. "I'm getting tired of worrying about her and her discovering the truth first."

~*~

Andy ran forward when Shandra rode the horse out of the trees near the Lightning barn. "I've been watching for you," he said, grabbing the reins and leading her over to the corral.

"It was a beautiful ride." Her jingle dress was hitched nearly up to her waist from trying not to sit on the metal cone shapes and flatten them. She stepped into the left stirrup, slid her dress down and placed her right foot on the ground. "How soon can we head back to the powwow grounds? I know your mom and the twins are worrying about me."

"We're set to go. Millie talked Scott into coming with us." He leaned closer. "Logan told me about Marian. Millie thought it best to keep Scott away from here for a bit."

"Good thinking. Any chance Millie would have some clothes I can change into and get out of this dress?" Shandra loved the dress but it was restrictive.

"You can ask. Here she comes." Andy led the horse over to the barn and unsaddled it.

"Shandra, are you okay? Do you need anything?" Millie put a hand on her arm.

"Would you happen to have a change of clothes I could wear back to the powwow? I don't want to smash anymore jingles on this dress while sitting in the car."

Millie took her by the arm. "Yes. Come on. And I'll get you something with sugar. You've had an awful ordeal."

Scott stood by the front door as Millie led Shandra inside.

Chapter Twenty-seven

"Are you sure you want to dance? You've had a terrible day," Aunt Jo said, unrolling another jingle dress from a leather roll.

"Yes. I came here to dance. I missed Mia and Jayden earlier today, I'm not going to miss them tonight and I need to dance for me." Shandra stared at the dress. "Why does that look familiar?"

"That picture of my mother in the living room?" Aunt Jo hinted.

"This is Grandmother's jingle dress?" Tears filled Shandra's eyes. She would not only be dancing to heal her time spent away from her family and the loss of her grandmother before she knew her well, but she would be wearing her grandmother's dress.

"Yes. And she would be proud to have you wear it." Tears glistened in Aunt Jo's eyes. "She so loved you and wished to see you. This would be a wonderful tribute to her and her love for you."

"I wish I had known sooner." They embraced and cried.

The teepee flap slapped against the side. "Are you hurt?" Jayden asked.

"No. I'm fine. Better than fine." Shandra swiped at the tears and her nose and smiled at Aunt Jo. "I'll be out in a few minutes. You and Mia wait for me by the campfire."

"You're sure you're okay?" He questioned more softly.

Shandra crossed the narrow space between them and gave him a hug. "I'm fine. They were happy tears. Ryan can tell you all about them later."

Jayden stared at her for a couple of seconds more then ran out of the teepee.

"Those two are good for you," Aunt Jo said.

"Yes, they are."

~*~

Ryan was tired, but glad he'd made it back to the powwow grounds in time to watch Mia and Shandra dance. He stood beside Andy, Millie, Coop, Sandy, and a distracted Scott, who'd tried to get him to say what had happened to Marian. All Ryan told him; she was at the police station being questioned.

The drummers circling the large drum, beat a steady cadence and the singing started. The women and girls began the distinctive step that made the silver cones on their dresses jingle and dance. They were light on their feet, dancing to the beat of the drum. The colors were bright and the concentration on the smaller children's face made him smile. He found Mia. She was smiling and keeping her feet to the beat of the drums. Scanning the women, his gaze landed on Shandra. She danced at the edge, her steps light, her toes pointed, her eyes on some point ahead of her. A sad smile tipped her lips.

"She's wearing Grandmother's dress," Coop said, pulling Ryan's attention from his wife.

"Her grandmother's dress?" No wonder she appeared melancholy.

"Mom said they both cried tears as Shandra put it on." Coop slapped a hand on his shoulder. "Be ready for an emotional night."

"I will." His phone vibrated. Logan.
Call when you finish watching the dancing.
Copy.

He returned his attention to the two women who held his heart.

~*~

Shandra walked out of the arbor holding Mia's hand. The dance had been what she'd needed after the events of this week. Wearing Grandmother's dress, she'd felt as if the woman was with her as she danced and thanked the Creator for all the wonderful things in her life. All the bad had led her to where she was now.

Ryan walked up to her, kissed her cheek and hugged Mia. "You two looked beautiful out there."

Mia giggled.

Shandra smiled back at her husband. "I can't describe the feeling, but we'll be back here next year, won't we?" she asked Mia.

"Yes!"

"I'm glad to hear that. Let's find a spot to watch Jayden and Andy." Ryan led them over to where the Higheagle-Elwood families were gathered to watch the dancers.

Jayden mimicked everything Andy did. It was fun watching his colorful strings bounce and sway like the grass as they danced.

At the end of the grass dance, Andy brought Jayden up to them. "I think he's had enough for one day."

"We all have. Thank you for bringing him to us," Shandra said, smiling at her cousin. "We'll see you all in the morning before we head home."

"Good night!" called out various family members as Ryan escorted his family back to the teepee.

When everyone had their pajamas on and were settled down for the night, Ryan whispered, "I need to call Logan. I'll be right back."

"Just don't wander off," she said and yawned.

"I won't." He walked out of the teepee and scrolled down his contacts for Logan. It rang once and the tribal officer answered.

"You wanted me to call?"

"I think we have this all sorted out. Pretty much what Shandra said at the shack. Marian knew Nathan, learned about the ranch, decided Scott would be a better way to get the ranch than Nathan, only to discover Nathan had more chance of getting the whole thing before Lucille started talking about a will. She was looking for the will when Lucille walked in on her. When Lucille wouldn't tell her where the will was, Marian got mad and choked her. Then sent Nathan looking for the will. By that time Geri showed up trying to figure out what was happening. Nathan will be held on attempted murder, Marian on murder charges, and Geri an accessory to attempted murder. Oh, and the kidnapping of Shandra. Who by the way, I need to come down and give us a statement."

"Can we do that in the morning before we leave?" Ryan asked. "She's exhausted."

"Tomorrow morning will be fine. See you both then."

Ryan ended the call and stood a moment, taking in the stars and the moon. He thanked whichever deity or guardian spirit that had kept his wife safe today, giving them many more years together.

Chapter Twenty-eight

The barbecue grill was smoking as Ryan tended the burgers and fries. The twins and Sheba were playing with two-year-old Donny Treat, Maxwell and Ruthie's son, and one-year-old Alexie, Alex and Miranda's daughter. The children's parents, along with Ted and Naomi Norton, were over for a summer barbecue. They gathered at one or the other's house once a month during the summer on a weekend.

"How was the powwow?" Ruthie asked. She'd spent her teen years with a Native American family.

"If you left out the murder we became caught up in, it was wonderful," Shandra said. And she meant it. Connecting with more of her family and building an even better connection with others had filled the emptiness she'd had for a long time.

"I danced the Jingle Dance." Mia stood up and began showing off her footwork.

"You're good!" Miranda said.

"Thank you! I learned it from Aunt Jo." She

glanced bashfully over at Shandra. "And Mom."

Shandra stared at Mia.

"Did I say something wrong?" she asked quietly.

"No! There is not another name I'd rather be called." She scooped up the child and hugged her.

"What about the one you got at the naming ceremony?" Jayden asked. Then he tried to pronounce the name in Nez Perce.

Everyone laughed.

"That isn't quite how you say it. But it means Lost One Follows Heart," Ryan said.

"That fits perfectly!" Naomi exclaimed.

"Yes, it does," added Ruthie.

"I'm glad you all think so, because I'm stuck with it. And because of my spirit guardian," Shandra faced Ryan. "I am no longer helping you with your police work. I have two children who need me more than you need me to help you."

Ryan put his arms around her. "I'm glad to hear that. I can sleep better knowing you will be staying out of danger."

Shandra kissed her husband. "It smells like you need to tend to those burgers."

Lil came around the side of the house. "I thought you kids wanted to ride Cookies and Cream? I got them all saddled and waitin'." The gruff woman who was Shandra's employee, walked up to Donny. "You mind if we give him a round or two on the horses?" she asked Ruthie.

"I think Donny would love that. And I'm coming along to take pictures." Ruthie stood.

"I'd love to see that, too," Miranda said, picking up Alexie.

Pretty soon only Shandra and Ryan stood on the back patio. He slipped his arms around her. "Did you mean what you said about no longer helping with my cases?"

"I did. Grandmother no longer comes in my dreams because I am doing what I'm supposed to do. Take care of Mia and Jayden. Maybe someday, when they are grown and I am at a loss for what to do, she'll return. Until then, I'm content to be your wife, their mother, and a potter. No more detective work for me."

Sheba ran out of the trees behind the house, turned around, and stretched her front legs out with her backside and tail in the air, like playing with something. Shandra peered beyond her into the trees and her heart stuttered. A silver wolf turned, disappearing into the trees. Grandmother may have left, but her wyakin would be with her.

~*~

Thank you for reading ***Vanishing Dream.*** If you haven't already figured it out, this is the last book in this series. After giving Ryan and Shandra the twins, I realized Shandra's character would look foolish running around putting her life in danger when there were children relying on her.

However, as I hinted at the end, there could be a reprisal of the series when the twins are grown and Shandra finds herself with an empty nest and Ryan is the Sheriff.

Specific information to this story I want to share: A vision quest is not something that is practiced in the present day. I implemented the quest into my story to help show my character's shift in attitude toward helping with murder investigations. It was one of the clues to show this series was ending and Shandra's change of attitude toward sleuthing.

If you are on my newsletter list or follow me on Facebook, you'll know that I am currently working on a new mystery series, Spotted Pony Casino Mysteries. It will be along the lines of the Shandra books, only the main character isn't Native American. She grew up on the reservation and lives and works there in the books.

Also, keep an eye out for the next Gabriel Hawke novel. Hawke will continue tracking and following murder leads for a while yet. I have a list of twenty plus animals I can use in titles.

As always, if you enjoyed this book, please leave a review. It is the best way to thank an author for an enjoyable read. I love to hear from fans. You can contact me through my website, blog, or newsletter.

All my work has Western or Native American elements in them along with hints of humor and engaging characters. My husband and I raise alfalfa hay in rural eastern Oregon. Riding horses and battling rattlesnakes, I not only write the western lifestyle, I live it.

You can contact or follow me at these places:

Website: http://www.patyjager.net
Blog: https://writingintothesunset.net/
FB Page: https://www.facebook.com/PatyJagerAuthor/
Amazon: https://www.amazon.com/Paty-Jager/e/B002I7M0VK
Pinterest: https://www.pinterest.com/patyjag/
Twitter: https://twitter.com/patyjag
Goodreads:
http://www.goodreads.com/author/show/1005334.Paty_Jager
Newsletter- Mystery: https://bit.ly/2IhmWcm
Bookbub - https://www.bookbub.com/authors/paty-jager

Thank you for purchasing this Windtree Press publication.
For other books of the heart, please visit our website
at www.windtreepress.com.

For questions or more information contact us
at info@windtreepress.com.

Windtree Press
www.windtreepress.com

Hillsboro, OR 97124

CPSIA information can be obtained
at www.ICGtesting.com
Printed in the USA
BVHW061119090222
628495BV00009B/944

9 781952 447693